G. P. PUTNAM'S SONS

A division of Penguin Young Readers Group. Published by The Penguin Group.
Penguin Group (USA) Inc., 375 Hudson Street, New York, NY 10014, U.S.A.
Penguin Group (Canada), 90 Eglinton Avenue East, Suite 700, Toronto,
Ontario, Canada M4P 2Y3 (a division of Pearson Penguin Canada Inc.).
Penguin Books Ltd, 80 Strand, London WC2R 0RL, England.
Penguin Ireland, 25 St. Stephen's Green, Dublin 2, Ireland (a division of Penguin Books Ltd.).
Penguin Group (Australia), 250 Camberwell Road, Camberwell, Victoria 3124, Australia
(a division of Pearson Australia Group Pty Ltd). Penguin Books India Pvt Ltd,
11 Community Centre, Panchsheel Park, New Delhi - 110 017, India.
Penguin Group (NZ), Cnr Airborne and Rosedale Roads, Albany, Auckland 1310, New Zealand
(a division of Pearson New Zealand Ltd).
Penguin Books (South Africa) (Pty) Ltd, 24 Sturdee Avenue, Rosebank, Johannesburg 2196,
South Africa. Penguin Books Ltd, Registered Offices: 80 Strand, London WC2R 0RL, England.

Design by Marikka Tamura. Text set in Folio Medium and Baskerville Book.
Library of Congress Cataloging-in-Publication Data
Richards, Justin. Ghost soldiers / by Justin Richards. p. cm. – (The Invisible Detective)
Summary: While investigating a haunted house, the Cannoniers discover a group of scientists
who are creating an army of indestructible mutant soldiers to fight the Germans in
pre–World War II London. [1. Monsters–Fiction. 2. Haunted houses–Fiction. 3. London
(England)–History–20th century–Fiction. 4. England–History–20th century–Fiction.
5. Horror stories. 6. Mystery and detective stories.]
I. Title. PZ7.R386Gho 2006 [Fic]–dc22 2005013280
ISBN 0-399-24500-6
1 3 5 7 9 10 8 6 4 2
First Impression

WITHDRAWN

W9-BIQ-363

The INVISIBLE DETECTIVE

GHOST SOLDIERS

by Justin Richards

SLEUTH
PUTNAM

For Mum—who worried about the goldfish . . .

CHAPTER 1

November 1936 was a cold month, but it was not the chill winter air that made Ed Simkins shiver.

The soldier was standing outside the empty house when he returned. Simkins had been sleeping there for the past week. It didn't matter to him that the place was supposed to be haunted. Or that the windows were broken and the floors rotting away. It kept out the worst of the winter and gave him a roof over his head. And if there were lights and noises and things that went bump in the night, then the cheap gin kept them away.

But even through his tired, blurred eyes he could see the soldier's silhouette in the doorway. Standing, as if on guard, outside the house. His house. At least, it was his as much as it was anyone else's.

Simkins recognized the khaki uniform from his days in the trenches. Nearly twenty years ago . . . So much had changed since then. But even before he managed to focus on the soldier, he could tell there was something odd about it. Sentries never stood that still. Not once did the soldier look around, or try to stamp some life back into his cold feet, or shift the weight of the pack he carried on his back.

In fact, now that he came to look at it, the shape of the pack was somehow wrong, skewed. You needed the weight at the top, over your shoulders, not bulging lower down.

Most worrying, Simkins realized, was that while he himself was breathing out a misty fog of air, the soldier in the doorway was not. As if he was not breathing at all.

Simkins took a hesitant step toward the house, toward the figure. When there was still no movement, he crossed the road with more confidence. Of course–it was not real at all. It was a waxwork or a shop dummy. That was why it was so still, why the pack was wrong, why no breath came from the lifeless lips. He chuckled to himself, shaking his head at his own foolishness as he started up the short path to the door.

Then the soldier turned and looked at him. The pale glow from the nearest streetlight illuminated the soldier's head as it angled toward him. Simkins stopped halfway up the path, anchored to the spot with pure terror as he saw what was under the helmet. Where there should have been a face.

The creature that was dressed as a soldier stepped down on to the path. There was a warm mist now, but not from its mouth. It seemed to emerge from every joint, every opening in the stained uniform. The hissing that Simkins could hear reminded him of the hydraulics of a gun platform. Was it the sound of the thing moving or of the mist that wreathed it? Or was it Simkins's own ragged breath as he finally managed to focus his mind on what was happening?

He turned and ran for his life.

. . .

"That's quite a story, Mr. Simkins," the Invisible Detective said. His voice was rich and mellow. A pale hand appeared for the briefest moment from the other side of the armchair, as if to punctuate his words. "What, may I ask, happened next?"

Brandon Lake, the Invisible Detective, was seated in the armchair and the chair was turned toward the wall. He never faced his audience. Nobody ever saw Brandon Lake. Nobody saw him arrive at the consulting sessions he held every Monday evening and nobody saw him leave. All that was ever visible was the hand and the vague shape of a figure in the chair in the dimly lit upstairs room above a locksmith's on Cannon Street. That was why he was called the Invisible Detective.

The main window of the room was bowed and the curtain cut straight across, so that there was a small area before the window. In this space, Jonny Levin and Meg Wallace struggled to hear Simkins as he blurted out his story in fits and starts of breathless memory. The sound of the rain was louder here and Flinch had given up trying to catch the words. She was sitting cross-legged on the floor, fidgeting impatiently.

Flinch was a small girl with long blond hair that was matted and dirty. She was perhaps twelve, perhaps older—she did not know. Flinch had lived on the streets for as long as anyone could remember. Now her home was an abandoned carpet warehouse on a corner of Cannon Street. Jonny and Meg were two of her best friends.

Jonny was a thin thirteen-year-old with short black hair. He was holding a fishing rod that he used to flick messages across to the armchair when necessary.

"Is he telling the truth?" Jonny asked Meg. If Simkins was lying, then the detective should know.

Meg shook her head, sending her long auburn curls into a frenzy of movement. "He's not lying," she murmured. "But it doesn't follow that what he says actually happened."

"What do you mean?"

"Can't you smell the drink?"

Simkins was standing close to the curtain, and now that Meg mentioned it, Jonny realized he could detect the stale, oddly dry smell of spirits.

"I ran," Simkins was saying. "Wouldn't you?" There was a rasp of drawn-in breath. "Came after me it did. That thing. Arms out, fingers snapping. Like metal they were. Metal gloves or something. Coming for me, like metal claws reaching for my throat."

Jonny could almost hear the man shudder.

"Not the only thing that's reached your throat, is it, Ed?" someone called out from the back of the room. There was an undercurrent of laughter at this.

"Good story, Ed," someone else said, perhaps emboldened by the first person. "One of your best."

"Yeah," the first voice called out again. "You remember

that time you was chased by a big blue bear? Bet that had claws." There was louder laughter at this. Evidently many of them knew the story. But that did not deter the speaker from delivering his punch line. "Turned out to be Constable Wilkins after you for drunk and disorderly."

"God rest his poor soul," a third voice muttered.

"I must admit . . . ," said the distinctive voice of Brandon Lake, causing everyone to quiet down again. "I must admit that there would seem to be a fairly straightforward solution to this particular case." He paused before adding, "Should we call it 'a case of spirits,' perhaps?"

The whole room erupted at this. Jonny was aware of Simkins trying to make himself heard above the hubbub: "I know what I seen. Really I do." But the hilarity continued, punctuated by the sound of footsteps stamping toward the stairs at the back of the room. Simkins's voice was fainter as he said, "I thought the Invisible Detective would help. No one else will, not the coppers, not no one. And that thing's still after me."

Nobody seemed willing to risk asking the Invisible Detective a serious question after Ed Simkins's performance. People were still laughing and joking as they left.

When the room was empty, Meg and Jonny emerged from behind the curtains and Jonny went to count the money. Everyone who had a question for the detective was supposed to leave sixpence in a tin by the stairs. Meg stood watching him, her arms folded and her face set.

"He really did believe it," she said. "That's what drink does to a man."

Flinch skipped happily across the room, delighted not to have to sit still any longer. She held her hands out to the Invisible Detective and he took them, allowing himself to be heaved out of the armchair.

"Thanks, Flinch." The detective's voice was lighter, younger, as he threw off his oversized coat. But, then, the Invisible Detective was not Brandon Lake at all—there was no such person. It was Art Drake, fourteen years old and leader of the Cannoniers. The other Cannoniers—Jonny, Meg and Flinch—gathered around him.

"What about Sozzled Ed's story, then?" Art asked them. "He should have been here last week and told it for Halloween."

There was much laughter at that. After all, they knew that even if Ed Simkins had actually seen something, it was not going to have been a ghost soldier with metal gloves.

It was Friday before Art thought about Ed Simkins's story again. He had given up waiting for his father to get home from work and was sitting in the kitchen, finishing his tea. Just as he rose to tidy things up, he heard the front door open.

"Sorry about that," his dad said, coming in and immediately setting the kettle on the stove. "I was just leaving Scotland Yard when something came up."

"Anything interesting?" Art asked.

His dad sighed. "Interesting, but not pleasant. Local drunk found dead in the gutter."

"That's not a detective matter, is it?"

"Not usually," Detective Sergeant Peter Drake agreed. "Sozzled Ed, that's what they called him locally."

"Ed Simkins?"

"That's right." His dad was surprised. "You knew him?"

Art shrugged. "Knew of him. Heard he told some pretty wild stories."

"Not anymore." Peter Drake clicked his tongue. "Murdered. Probably for the price of a drink, knowing the company he kept. Throat torn out, poor chap. Odd thing, though . . ." He paused as the kettle started to whistle. He lifted it off the heat, protecting his hand with a folded tea towel.

"What was odd?" Art asked. He had a cold, numb feeling in the pit of his stomach.

"I don't think you want to know." His dad smiled. "Especially after you've just eaten."

"No, tell me."

"The pathologist said it looked as if he'd been attacked by something with claws, except the marks were too regular. Machined. As if . . ."

"As if," Art suggested, "the claws were made of metal?"

And his dad nodded.

It was strange, Arthur Drake thought, how he no longer felt embarrassed about visiting his grandfather in the home. The television was on, but only his dad was watching—football.

Arthur and Grandad sat on the other side of the small room, talking quietly. Grandad had a newspaper on his lap folded to the crossword. But neither of them was very interested in the clues.

Perhaps it was not so strange that they were now such friends, Arthur decided. After all, they had faced a monster together. But he still found it hard to think of his grandfather as young—as young as Arthur himself was now. Hard to think of him as Art, the Invisible Detective, all those years ago, back in the 1930s.

It was even more difficult because Arthur was himself—somehow—that Art as well. In his dreams, or when he stared deep into the strange oval stone he had found at Bessemer's Paranormal Puppet Show. . . . No, he had to remind himself, it was Art—Grandad—who had found the stone. Arthur had been given it by the old man who owned the antiques shop on Cannon Street that he passed on the way to school.

He could remember that day as if it were yesterday. He could remember sheltering in the shop from the rain and the old man giving him the stone. He had also given Arthur a handwritten notebook—handwritten, it seemed, in his own writing. It was the casebook of the Invisible Detective. He could remember how surprised he had been to see his own name signed in it and his own address. Now, of course, he knew it was Grandad's. But even so . . .

"I read about the ghost soldiers last night," Arthur said quietly.

Grandad nodded. "And do you remember any of it?" he asked with amusement.

Arthur grinned back. Grandad knew that often when he read the cases in the book, he then forgot them. It was as if he was somehow not allowed to remember the events until the time was right. He could not recall the Shadow Beast until he and Grandad had faced their own monster. "Yes, I re-member," he said. "And I was wondering—what really hap-pened to Algie?"

Grandad shrugged. "I wish I knew for sure. I've often wondered that myself. I hope . . ." His cracked voice tailed off. He coughed a dry hoarse cough before going on. "But it's no use hoping. Not now. Not after so long and after so many other things have happened. It can't make any differ-ence, can it?"

"I suppose not."

"Oh, will you look at that?" Arthur's father cried from across the room. He glanced around at them for support. "Penalty at least."

"At least," Arthur agreed, without looking.

"Seemed fair enough to me," Grandad said, his eyes widening slightly with amusement.

But Arthur's dad was already engrossed in the match again.

"Do you know anything about websites?" Arthur asked. "The Internet and stuff?"

"Computers? Not much. What they are, a little of what they can do. The web's like an online library, isn't it?"

"Well . . ."

"Why do you ask? Your father thinking of getting me a computer, is he?"

Arthur laughed. "I don't know. Do you want one?"

Grandad shook his head. "I don't think so. You tell me."

"You might actually. There's this website—like a page you can look up. But it's called the Invisible Detective."

"Is it now?" Grandad turned slightly, interested.

"There's a bit about the original Invisible Detective. Well, you know—the official story if you like. But mainly you type in questions and they send you back answers by e-mail. It says there's some bank of computers doing it. Searching through the Internet for stuff that matches your question and sending it on to you."

"Computerized librarian?"

"Sort of. Only . . . Only I get weird stuff sent to me," Arthur confessed. "This Invisible-Detective.com site sent me an e-mail saying, 'Ask me about the Shadow Beast' once."

Grandad frowned. "Did it now?"

"So I thought—well, I thought maybe you had something to do with it. You or one of the other Cannoniers—Meg or Jonny or Flinch."

Grandad shook his head. "It's a funny thing, age, you know. Back then, when we dealt with the Shadow Beast, or the ghost soldiers, I was a bit older than Meg and Jonny, and much older than Flinch. But now . . . Well, time is a great leveler. I don't think any of us is up to organizing a website these days, Arthur. It's enough of an effort just filling in the crossword." He lifted his gnarled hand, the ballpoint pen held awkwardly between his arthritic fingers.

Arthur was not sure what to say to this. But he was saved as the referee blew the final whistle and Dad switched off the television in disgust.

"That lot couldn't beat your school team, Arthur." He checked his watch. "We must go."

"Off to the fireworks tonight," Arthur said.

"The big display at Sydenham," Dad explained. "Crystal Palace Park. You want to come? It shouldn't be that cold."

Grandad smiled and shook his head. "After my bedtime, I expect. Anyway," he went on, looking meaningfully at Arthur, "I've seen fireworks there before."

CHAPTER 2

"As you are all no doubt aware," the Invisible Detective told his audience, "Mr. Simkins will sadly not be with us today."

There were murmurs from around the room. Everyone had heard how Simkins had been found dead, and while the details might not have been made public, most people knew them anyway. News, especially bad news, traveled quickly. Jonny knew that Art was hoping to gloss over the death and move quickly on to this week's questions. They had discussed it the previous afternoon at the den. This was a police matter, Art had told them. None of them disagreed, though Jonny was disappointed that they were giving up on a potential adventure before they had even started.

Flinch had also been disappointed, Jonny could tell. Her mouth twitched at the edges and she looked away. That was one of the reasons she had not come to this session and was staying back at the den. But Meg had nodded and said it was sensible. "Sensible" was a good description of Meg. She was the most down to earth of them all. Even Art was given to occasional flights of fancy and moments of silliness, but Meg was always sensible.

Someone cleared his throat at the back of the room. Jonny and Meg both tried to peer around the curtain to see who it was. When he spoke, they recognized the voice of Albert Norris, the bartender at the Dog and Goose.

"We all know that Sozzled Ed was murdered," Norris said. "And I think we'd like to know what you're going to do about it."

There was a short pause and Jonny could imagine Art, huddled inside the massive coat of the Invisible Detective, wondering what to say to this.

"Do?" the detective's voice eventually answered. "This is, of course, a police matter. Regrettable and sad, but Scotland Yard's finest are on the case."

Jonny caught a hint of pride in Art's disguised tone at this—his father was the officer in charge of the investigation.

"Regrettable?" Norris barked back. "Regrettable?" His anger was obvious. "Mr. Lake, sir, I don't like admitting it any more than you do, but a few of us were talking down at the Dog last night."

"Oh?"

"Ed Simkins enjoyed his drink and no mistake. Had a fair few down at the Dog on occasion, I can tell you. But that don't excuse it. Not one bit."

"I'm sorry, Mr. Norris." The Invisible Detective sounded slightly pained. "I am not sure that I entirely understand your meaning."

"My meaning, sir, is that you are the Invisible Detective, right?"

"Right," the detective agreed, slightly hesitantly.

"And people come to you for help, right." This time it was not a question, and Norris went on without pausing for confirmation. "And Ed Simkins, he came to you for help last week. Now, I admit we all had a bit of a laugh, none of us believed his story. Cried wolf a few times too often has Sozzled Ed, we all know that."

"But this time he was right," the detective said slowly. Jonny could almost hear Art's brain working as he spoke. "He came to me for help and now he is dead. Is that it?"

Jonny could just make out a silhouette that might be Norris shuffling uncomfortably in the gloom beyond the curtains. "In a nutshell. It ain't just me thinks that," he added quickly.

"Came here for help he did," a woman's voice, high-pitched with nervous embarrassment, agreed. "And you just made a joke of it, sir, if you don't mind me saying so. . . ." The voice tailed off, as if the woman was afraid she might have gone too far.

There was an awkward pause before the Invisible Detective spoke again. " 'A case of spirits,' I think I said." They could all hear the sigh that followed. "You are right, of course, Mr. Norris. And the rest of you. We all assumed that Mr. Simkins had been the worse for drink and imagined he was in danger. Now, at the very least, it seems there may have been some foundation to his anxiety. And, at worst, he was absolutely right."

"It could just be a coincidence," Norris admitted, as if, having got this far, he was unwilling to press the point.

"Just so, but I agree that we owe it to Mr. Simkins to find out."

"Thank you, sir." There was relief in Norris's voice. "He had no next of kin, no family at all, did Ed. The police came to me to ask what to do with his possessions."

"Possessions?" someone chuckled close to the curtain. "Ed—possessions? Half-empty bottle, was it?"

Norris ignored them. "Course, he didn't have much. His clothes were only good for burning. But he had thrupence ha'penny in his pocket. Policeman said to see it went to a good cause. Reckon this is as good as any. It ain't sixpence," Norris apologized, "but I'll leave it in the tin."

"Thank you, Mr. Norris," the Invisible Detective said. "You may rest assured that it will indeed go to a good cause. And I promise you that I shall give this case—whether it be one of coincidence, murder or spirits—my fullest attention."

Back at the den, the Cannoniers sat around and waited for Art to speak. They had not talked about what had happened until they got back to the disused warehouse with its dusty, rotting rolls of carpet. Then Jonny had told Flinch all about the session and what Albert Norris had said. Art could see her eyes widening with excitement and anticipation as Jonny spoke.

He could also see that Meg was less than happy. She rarely seemed in good humor anyway, but the way she had her arms tightly folded and her lips pressed together made him wary.

"I had to agree," Art told her quietly as Jonny finished relating events to Flinch.

"Did you?"

Meg's voice cut across the warehouse and made Jonny and Flinch turn to look. They slowly came over to join the two older children.

"Well, yes. What was I supposed to do?" Art demanded. "Tell him that we all thought Ed Simkins was drunk and imagining things?"

"He was."

"And that it was quite right and proper to make a joke of it, even though he really was in danger and now he's dead?"

But Meg was not listening. The light from the street outside shone through a murky broken window, making her auburn hair shine as if it were on fire. "What is the point of us deciding things if you go and change your mind? What's the point of Cannoniers' meetings if Art Drake and the Invisible Detective just decide to do whatever they want anyway?"

"That's not fair," Jonny said. But he said it quietly and without catching Meg's eye.

"It is fair," Art said loudly. He was pleased to see that Meg looked surprised. "It is fair," he said again, more calmly and quietly. "We should discuss these things. But that wasn't really possible in the session just now, was it?"

Meg said nothing, but he could tell that she appreciated the point.

"So let's discuss it now," Art said. "We're a team. All of us are the Invisible Detective—not just me. But sometimes I have to do things on the spur of the moment, on behalf of us all. I'm sorry, but that's how it is."

He sat down on a battered roll of threadbare carpet. He could smell the powdery, smoky odor of the dust as Meg sat down next to him.

"What do we need to discuss?" Flinch wanted to know, sitting cross-legged on the floor in front of them.

Jonny flopped down beside her.

"Well, first of all, I agreed—on our behalf—to look into Ed Simkins's murder. That could just mean that I ask Dad what's going on and then the Invisible Detective reports that back. Or as much as is proper." Art looked around at his friends, all of them watching him attentively. "Or we could do a little investigating of our own."

"Oh, yes," Flinch said quickly. "Though I s'pose we could go to Charlie."

"He wouldn't be interested," Jonny said.

Charlie—Lord Fotherington—was a friend of theirs who had been a great help on a previous case. But he was bound to be busy on government business.

Art smiled. "We might mention it next time he joins us for tea at the station café," he said. "But before we decide what to do, I'd like to know whether Meg is upset because she thinks we should leave well alone or because we made a decision that we might be about to change."

Meg still had her arms folded, but her expression was more relaxed. "As long as we all decide together," she said. "That's all. It might be dangerous, I suppose. But we've faced worse."

Flinch shivered at the comment, obviously recalling their past adventures.

"We should investigate," Jonny said. "That's what I think. There's a mystery and we solve mysteries. That's what the Invisible Detective does. Like Albert Norris said, Sozzled Ed came to us for help and he didn't get it. We owe it to him."

Art nodded. "That's how I feel, I have to admit. I hadn't thought of it like that till it was pointed out this evening. But, yes, we owe Ed Simkins."

He looked at Meg. They were all looking at Meg.

"All right," she said. She still looked sullen, but then she smiled. It was just a small smile, but it transformed her whole face. "After all, we've got his thrupence ha'penny."

While he was well known in the Cannon Street area, Ed Simkins seemed to have spent most of his time south of the river. From listening to the discussions of the people leaving the Invisible Detective session, Art and the others knew that he was based in and around Borough—just across Southwark Bridge. From Simkins's own story, they knew he had been sleeping in an empty house on Jursall Street. Number 7.

Meg wanted to get home by nine, she said. Nobody asked her why. Art and Jonny could stay out a bit later, and Flinch had no need to be anywhere at any time unless she wanted.

"How about if Meg and I look around Borough and ask a few questions?" Jonny suggested. "I can get Meg home, then nip back if there's anything we want to follow up on tonight."

"Good idea," Art said. "If Meg's agreeable." He knew that Jonny could run back to Borough in less time than it took him to walk from the den to Cannon Street station. "Flinch and I will take a look at the house where Simkins says he saw the ghost soldier or whatever it really was."

Flinch's eyes widened. "Ghosts?"

"Shadows, more likely," Meg told her. "Or spirits, as Art said. The sort that come in a bottle."

"Oh." It was difficult to tell if Flinch was relieved or disappointed.

As Art and Flinch stood across the street from the house in the chilly dark of the November evening, Art could see that she was shivering beneath her coat. The coat had been Meg's. It was too big for Flinch and worn almost through at the cuffs and elbows. But in the foggy gloom it made the girl seem more grown up. Almost respectable.

Art squeezed her hand. "It does look a bit spooky, doesn't it? That's probably all there is to it."

The house was set back slightly from the road. What garden there was had been left to get overgrown and grass was matted across the slabbed pathway that led to the front door. There were a couple of steps up to a porch. They could not see the door itself, as it was in shadow. But the dim glow from the nearest streetlamp glinted on the broken glass of the window above the door.

There were two large bay windows on each of the two floors of the house. All of them had at least one broken pane, and the window to the left of the door was boarded up with plywood. A small window above the porch was the only one that remained intact. With the steps leading up to the porch cracked across so they looked like teeth, the empty bay windows of the upper story were like the dark eyes of a skull. Missing tiles on the roof gave texture to what looked like remnants of hair.

"What do you think?" Art asked.

"Like you said, spooky." Flinch continued to stare at the house for a few moments before she added, "Let's go inside."

Art laughed. "You sure?"

Before Flinch could answer, they heard footsteps. The street had been deserted the whole time they had been there. There were not many houses facing the street. Most had their front doors in the next road and back gardens with rotting gates giving out on Jursall Street. The few houses there were seemed to be empty and one was completely boarded up.

Art stepped back, drawing Flinch with him into the shadow of the wall. Someone was walking briskly along the street. They could see the silhouette against the wisps of evening fog as the figure approached. Whoever it was seemed to be in a hurry. Their feet were loud on the pavement.

As the figure came closer, Art could see that it was a woman. Her footsteps were loud because she had small heels that stamped down purposefully as she walked. When she passed under the streetlamp, he could see she was wearing a gray jacket over a gray skirt. Even her face seemed gray in the diffuse light. But her hair was as black as the night and cut very short. She paused for a moment and looked around. Her nose was a cruel beak, so that in profile she looked like a witch, Art thought. Satisfied that she was the only person on the street, she started off again, her pace quickening, her shoes like gunshots on the flagstones as she made her way quickly up the overgrown path and into the dark mouth of the porch.

For a moment the skull became a house as the door opened and light spilled out. Not much, just enough to illuminate the woman as she went inside. Then the door closed again and the house was once more a skull staring across the road at Art and Flinch.

"What's she doing in there?" Flinch wanted to know.

"Good question." Art considered. "Doesn't look like she's roughing it. Visiting, maybe?"

"Visiting who?"

"Yes, looks pretty deserted, doesn't it?"

As they were speaking, Art could see the pale progress of a lamp or flashlight through the ground-floor window to the right of the door. After a short while, the light faded.

"We'll wait for her to come out," Art decided, "then we'll nip inside and see what she's been up to. All right with you?"

Flinch nodded. "How long will she be?"

"Well, there can't be much to do in there. A few minutes at the most, I should think."

But Art was wrong. After an hour she had still not emerged. Flinch was stamping her feet and clapping her hands to keep warm. Art felt as though his legs had wandered off on their own—perhaps to find somewhere warm.

"Maybe something's happened to her in there?" Flinch suggested. Her voice was slightly husky with the thought. "Like it happened to Sozzled Ed."

Art had been thinking the same thing, but he did not want to frighten Flinch. "More likely she went out the back door," he said. "Still, it would do no harm to check."

The door was locked. A number 7 hung crookedly on a rusty nail alongside it. But the board on the window beside the door was loose at the bottom. Art was able to pull it away from the window frame just enough to allow Flinch to wriggle her way through. It was incredible how small a gap Flinch could negotiate. He watched as she eased her shoulders through the tiny slit between the stone mullion and the plywood, and tried not to wince as he heard the click when she dislocated her shoulder joints in order to fit through more easily.

Flinch's feet disappeared through the gap and Art let go of the plywood. It snapped back into place with a sharp crack and he looked around quickly to make sure no one was there to hear. After a short pause, he heard a key turn in the lock, followed by the sound of a bolt being drawn back, and then the front door opened to reveal Flinch's grubby but smiling face.

"Bolt's at the top," she said. "Had to get a chair to stand on."

Art carried the upright wooden chair back to the room Flinch had climbed into. The support strut between the back legs was broken, and the upholstered seat was dusty and worn almost through. The room seemed to have been a dining room a long time ago. The remains of a broken wooden table stood in the center, surrounded by the skeletal remains of chairs. Like sentries guarding an ancient monument, Art thought.

"Where do we start?" Flinch whispered. "Should we split up?"

"Let's stay together," Art suggested. "Just go through each room in turn."

The floorboards creaked as they walked. The light that

spilled in through the broken windows cast deep shadows across the walls and floor. If he had been asked to design a haunted house, Art thought, it would be exactly like this.

Some of the rooms were empty. Others had the broken, faded remains of furniture in them. The kitchen at the back of the house was covered in grime and dirt, but Art braved it to get to the back door. It was nailed shut—the woman could not have left that way.

Most of the windows too were locked. As they went through the ground floor, Art came to realize that the woman could not have left the house. She must still be inside. With them. He put his finger to his lips and whispered to Flinch to keep quiet.

The wooden door under the stairs—presumably to a cupboard or storage area—was locked and refused to move. It seemed to have survived the rot of time better than the rest of the house.

There was no carpet on the stairs, though torn threads of material still clung to the ornate metal grips that had once held the carpet in place. Every other step seemed to creak as it took their weight and the shadows at the top of the stairs seemed to deepen as they approached.

Once on the landing, Art chose the nearest doorway. The door was closed but opened easily as he turned the handle. It swung back with a protesting groan to reveal nothing but blackness beyond.

"Hello?" Art called cautiously. Wherever the woman

was, whatever she was doing, she must have heard them by now. "Are you all right? We were worried about you."

As if in answer, Art thought he could hear a whistling sound. High-pitched and very faint. He looked at Flinch, who shrugged. The sound came again, louder now. Flinch shrank back from it, but Art took a deep breath and stepped into the blackness.

Immediately the darkness came to life. He could feel it on his face, in his hair, flapping against his body. He could hear it shrieking and screaming at him as he invaded its space. There was a texture to the dark—black, leathery, dry and brittle—as it whipped around his face and clawed at him. The whole of the room was a swirling mass, the night come alive and attacking him.

Art stumbled back out of the room. He slapped at his face, feeling the blackness still there, clinging to him. He could see it in patches over his body—flapping, clawing, crawling. . . .

In an instant, Flinch ran to help, tearing with him at the bats and pulling them away. They flew in a blizzard around the landing before disappearing back into the darkened room where Art had disturbed them.

"You all right, Art?" Flinch asked, breathless. She was looking about her in fear, her breath short and ragged.

"I will be in a minute. Thanks, Flinch."

"Don't like bats," she confessed. "They're all right till you disturb them. There's some that live at the top of the den." She looked around again. "But they're frightened of us too, Meg says. Leave them alone and they'll keep away."

"Thanks, I'll remember that."

Art wiped at his face and felt a slick of blood on the back of his hand. One of the bats had scratched him. Maybe several had. But Flinch was right, he had startled them, frightened them. Not half as much as they had frightened him, though.

"I don't think that lady's here." Flinch was looking around again. Her large eyes caught the light, making her look suddenly startled and afraid. "Maybe she's a ghost."

Art wanted to tell her that was ridiculous, but he was still too shaken from his encounter with the bats. And at that exact moment there came a sound from somewhere below them. It seemed to emanate from the very foundations of the house. A roaring sound that grew in volume and intensity until the whole place seemed to be rumbling with laughter. From the top of the stairs, Art could see a strip of bright light working its flickering way across the hall floor—as if it had come in through the closed front door and was approaching the stairs. As if it was looking for them.

Flinch grabbed Art's arm and clung to him, shaking. Art stood frozen to the spot, watching the light as it climbed the stairs toward them, shimmering over the bare wood.

Then the rumbling laughter slowly died away and the light faded as if absorbed by the substance of the staircase itself.

"Come on," said Art. "Let's get out of here."

They ran down the stairs and out of the door. The cold night air whipped at their hair and faces and clothes as they ran down Jursall Street and toward Borough station.

Behind them the house watched through empty, boarded eyes.

The air was cold and damp. When Arthur breathed out, his breath added to the mist already hanging in the air.

"Not the best of weather for fireworks," Arthur's dad said, checking his watch. He had to leave by nine to get to work.

They were standing just inside the park gates, looking up Sydenham Hill. The rockets were being launched from the hill, bursting into stars and streams of colored light above them. Their shape was diffused by the mist, the sound deadened by the damp air. But it was spectacular nonetheless.

Close behind them, a small boy sitting on his father's shoulders shouted "Bang" every time there was an explosion.

"Hello, Arthur." The voice startled him. Not because it was loud—what with the fireworks and the "bang" boy, Arthur hardly heard it. But it was a voice he recognized.

Her long black hair was tied back in a ponytail hidden behind her, so it took Arthur a moment to be sure it was Sarah Bustle. "Hello," he said, aware that Dad had also turned to see who it was. "This is Sarah," he explained.

Dad's face was set in an expression that was part surprised, part puzzled. "Not Sarah Bustle?" He laughed, shaking his head in apparent disbelief. "My goodness, you've changed a bit since I last saw you."

She tilted her head to one side. "It has been a few years, Mr. Drake."

Arthur listened to the exchange with rising disbelief.

"How's your mum?" his dad asked.

"She's fine, thanks. I'll tell her you asked."

"Please do. Must be, what, three years? Paul was, let me see, two, I think."

"He's seven now."

Dad sighed. "I feel so old," he said in a resigned tone. He seemed to notice Arthur's expression. "I didn't realize you two were such friends."

"We go to school together," Arthur replied, not willing to commit to friendship as such.

"I'm in the year above Arthur," Sarah said. "But we see each other now and again." She smiled at Arthur, though he wasn't sure if that was because she was actually pleased or because she was making a joke of it. "Anyway, I'd better get back to my friends."

"Is your mother here?" Arthur's dad asked quickly.

Sarah shook her head. "At home with Paul. It's too late for him to be out."

"Remember me to her. We must get in touch again."

But Sarah was gone, fading into the misty crowd. Her departure was punctuated by an explosion of stars high above them. "Bang!"

Arthur was determined not to ask his father how he knew Sarah and her family. But he wanted to know. He shuffled his feet, watching his dad check his watch yet again.

"I have to leave at nine."

"I know. You said. You're on duty at the Yard."

But he wasn't listening. "Sarah Bustle," he said quietly. "Who'd have thought." Then, at last, he did explain. "I knew her father. Years ago. That's how I know Sarah's mother, Linda, of course. She was a computer programmer in the same department as Jeff when they met. But I haven't seen them for years. Not since Jeff . . . " He shrugged. "She still does something in that line. Or did. Busy woman. Be nice to get in touch again. Especially with you two being such friends."

"We're not 'such friends,' " Arthur said, his teeth gritted partly against the cold of the evening. "We're just . . . friends."

CHAPTER 3

It was getting late, and Jonny and Meg were having little success. Despite Meg's objections, Jonny had managed to persuade her into a pub in the next street to where Ed Simkins's body had been found.

"He wasn't called Sozzled Ed for nothing, you know," he told her.

Reluctantly, she accepted that asking about Simkins in the pub was a sensible idea. However, while he might have spent his last days in the area, Simkins did not seem to have been a regular at the pub. Someone recalled the bartender throwing out a man who might have been Simkins a week ago. But from what Meg and Jonny were able to gather, it could really have been anyone, as this was not an infrequent occurrence. Indeed, approaching the bartender had provoked a very similar response, especially when Meg countered his observations about their age with her own thoughts on the evils of alcohol. They left in a hurry, with no useful information.

It was Jonny's turn to be nervous now.

"It's not like his body is still there," Meg insisted.

Jonny shrugged, not wanting to appear so anxious. "I know. It's just that . . ." He wasn't sure what it was, but Meg put her hand on his shoulder as if she understood anyway.

"I don't like the idea of visiting a murder site either," she told him. "But it's the best place to look for clues, isn't it?"

alley, they peered cautiously along the road in the direction the two figures had taken.

There was a black car parked at the curb. The light was shining through from behind and two heads could be seen.

"That's them," Jonny said at once.

The car was pulling out. It turned in the road and started moving slowly away.

"We'd better follow them, I suppose."

"They're in a car," Meg said.

"So what?" He was not sure about ghost soldiers and strange men in top hats, but Jonny knew about cars. He knew about speed. "See if you can keep up."

He knew she couldn't and was surprised when Meg started to run. But at once he was ahead of her, sprinting after the taillights of the car as they faded in the misty evening.

"See you back at the den," he shouted.

The road swung around to the left in a shallow curve, and Jonny could see a narrow path between two rows of buildings that cut the corner. He sprinted along it, footsteps echoing off the brickwork. As he reached the other end and emerged onto the street again, the car was just passing. Jonny grinned and chased after it.

Luckily the car did not go far. Even Jonny would have had trouble keeping up had it sped away, or just taken a straight route. But the driver seemed to be making sure he was not

She stared Jonny straight in the eye. "It's what the Invisible Detective would do," she said.

Jonny took a deep breath. "OK, just a quick look. After all, you need to get home."

According to Art's dad, Simkins's body had been discovered in an alley just off the next street. Meg and Jonny found it without difficulty. A streetlamp at each end of the alley cast a dull glow across the cobblestones, but the light from one failed to meet the equivalent light from the other. It was in this dark area, between a factory and the back walls of a row of shops, that Sozzled Ed had been found.

A figure was walking toward them. The light shone around him, starkly framing his silhouette. Jonny almost yelped with surprise, but Meg pulled him quickly out of the way. Together they crouched in the shadow of the wall and watched the man approach.

"What's the problem?" Jonny asked in a whisper. He was embarrassed at being startled, but it was just a man walking down an alley. He was wearing, so far as Jonny could tell from the dark shape, a top hat and a heavy coat with the collar turned up, and he carried a cane.

"I don't know," Meg whispered back. "But I think I've seen him somewhere before."

Jonny stared hard into the light at the other end of the alley, but still he couldn't make out any details of the man. "Are you sure?"

"I said 'I think,' " Meg snapped in reply.

They shrank back again as the man reached the patch of darkness. Perhaps he had heard Meg, but for whatever reason he leaned forward, so that his face was illuminated by the last vestiges of light from their end of the alley. The man's complexion was swarthy and he had sideburns that reached down to the level of his chin. His hair was sticking out in tufts between his hat and the collar of his coat. The silver top of his cane caught the light as he moved it.

"Yes, that's him," Meg hissed. "Whoever it is."

Apparently satisfied that there was nobody watching him, the man turned away, looking into the darkness. And for the first time Jonny became aware that there was someone else with him—someone who had been standing motionless in the darkness.

"Anything?" The man's voice seemed loud in the still of the night. If the other figure gave an answer, Jonny did not hear it. The man spoke again. "This should have been checked last week. Before the police were here. When that fool was dealt with." There was a slight frosting to the air as he breathed out heavily.

The man started walking back toward the far end of the alley. His footsteps were muffled by the night. In the distance a ship hooted on the river. When he was halfway along, the man turned.

"Well come on, then," he called to the darkness. "Have you no initiative of your own?"

At first Jonny thought that the unseen figure in the darkness was clearing its throat to answer. Then he thought

that what he could hear was distant machinery—f docks perhaps, or the ship he had just heard. It was mic, hissing hydraulic sound, followed by a thum thump, Jonny realized, of a foot hitting the c stones heavily.

Jonny glanced at Meg beside him. Her attention w cused on the alley. When she blinked and gasped, J looked back.

There was another figure now, moving slowly to the man. Like him, it was silhouetted against the ot streetlamp. The hissing thumping of its jerky movemen was joined now by a slavering sound. For the briefest m ment the figure's head turned slightly to the side and Jonn saw that it had a pronounced jaw. Then it turned away again and lurched forward another step.

The man did not wait for it to catch up with him but turned and strode off down the alley. The figure hurried after him, its movements jerky and uncoordinated. It seemed stooped and misshapen, like a hunchback. As it approached the light, Jonny could see that a faint mist seemed to accompany it, as if the fog of London was seeping from its joints. And he could see too that it was in uniform. What Jonny had thought was its hunched back was a heavy pack. It was a soldier.

"Come on! Quick!" Meg was on her feet and starting down the alley as soon as the figure turned at the bottom and disappeared from sight.

Reluctantly, Jonny went after her. At the end of the

being followed—not being followed by another car, rather than by the fastest kid in London town.

The car doubled back on itself several times. Occasionally it slowed or even stopped to let another vehicle overtake it. All of which allowed Jonny to take quicker ways and keep it within sight.

Eventually the car stopped once more. The headlights were turned off and the back door opened. The figure that seemed to be in army uniform got out ponderously. The driver wound down his window and spoke to it, though they were too far away for Jonny to hear what was said. Then the figure made its steady but measured way along the street. There were few houses. It took the short path up to the front of one of them.

Only when the figure had vanished inside did the car's headlights come on again. Jonny watched it pull away and vanish into the night. He did not try to follow this time. He was almost exhausted from the frantic chase, and in any case he ought to report back to the others at the den. He wanted to tell them about the strange figure that had let itself into a derelict house on Jursall Street—the same house that Art and Flinch had been investigating.

By nine o'clock the fireworks were over, finishing with a spectacular explosion of colored lights high above Sydenham Park. It was so impressive, the small boy neglected to shout "Bang"—or perhaps his voice was drowned out by the percussion.

Arthur and his father walked together back to the main road, joining the crowds who were already drifting away. Then Dad left Arthur to make his own way home.

Arthur joined a long line at the bus stop. Ahead of him he could see Sarah Bustle, but she did not look back and he did not like to call out. Although she had said she was with friends, she seemed to be alone. Perhaps her friends were taking another route home, or had a lift, or . . . Arthur wondered vaguely who Sarah's friends were as he stamped his cold feet and waited for the bus. Girls from school, probably. Boyfriend maybe. Not that he cared.

The line moved along as a double-decker bus came, but there was not room for everyone. People laughed and joked and waited patiently for the next one. When it arrived, Arthur just managed to get a seat. He did not see where Sarah went. Upstairs maybe. He was close to the door, wedged between a large woman with plastic carrier bags and a thin-faced man in a leather jacket who kept sniffing.

He watched the streetlights go by through the door, thinking of how much more interesting the light from the fireworks had been. In his mind's eye he could see a raging fire on the same site as he thought back through the latest case he had read of the Invisible Detective. . . . And before he knew it, he felt his head nod forward. He woke for a moment of clarity before it nodded forward again, and with the lulling movement of the bus he was soon asleep.

He woke briefly somewhere in Camberwell, judging by the road signs that blurred past. Then suddenly he was wide awake. The bus had stopped again and Sarah was getting off. He caught sight of her distinctive profile as she jumped down and started quickly along the pavement.

Immediately Arthur leaped up and followed. He didn't know exactly where she lived, but it was close to his own house—he saw her walking home sometimes from school. Had he already missed his stop? He stood on the pavement, looking around as the bus pulled away again.

Actually, he did not recognize the area at all. But there was a street name on the opposite corner—Lavington Street. It gave the area as Southwark. Southwark? He was miles away—the wrong side of the river. The area was quiet and he could see Sarah turning onto another street. Maybe she was meeting her friends at their house. Maybe they hadn't room in their car for her. Or something like that.

It was probably a half-hour walk home, but at least it was dry—a crisp, clear night now that the mist had lifted. If he found a main road, he would know where he was. So, because it was as good a direction as any to start in, Arthur followed Sarah.

He was just in time to see her turning off onto another, smaller street. It did not look promising, but he went on after her anyway. She was too far away to notice him probably.

But Arthur did not try to catch up with her. If she had seen him as soon as he stepped off the bus, maybe he could have explained, but now it would be hard to say that he wasn't following her—because he was. And he was not really sure why.

It might be something to do with the assured way she was walking. She looked so purposeful that Arthur was certain she was heading for somewhere in particular—somewhere close by. He was curious to know where. Having started to follow, and without hitting a main road or more likely route home, it was difficult to stop.

Until he turned another corner and found that Sarah had gone. The street ahead was empty. Along one side were simply the back gardens of the houses in the next street. What houses there were opposite seemed derelict and forgotten. As Arthur walked slowly along the street, searching in the gloom for any clue as to where Sarah might have gone, he passed several houses. Each looked cold and empty. The windows were either boarded up or broken, the paths overgrown, the roofs shedding tiles. . . .

He stopped at last, wondering whether to go on or to turn back. There was no light from any of the houses and even the streetlights seemed not to be working. Arthur glanced across at the house he had stopped outside. It was set slightly back from the road, up an overgrown path. A number 7 hung crookedly beside the door, illuminated for a moment by a stab of moonlight before fading back into the shadows of the porch as a cloud rolled in.

For some reason the house seemed familiar, though he was certain he had never seen it before. One of the ground-floor windows was boarded up and all the other windows had at least one broken pane. The dark upper windows looked like the eye sockets of a misshapen skull, the steps up to the porch its jagged, decaying teeth. . . .

Arthur shivered and turned back the way he had come. He must have been wrong. Sarah would not have come up here. She had taken another route. He paused at the end of the road. There was a sign attached to the ancient brick wall, but the letters had faded and a bush was growing up over it. Arthur leaned down and pushed the brittle branches aside, peering at the faint letters.

His heart seemed to miss a beat and he glanced instinctively back toward the skull house. Number 7. He wanted to go back, to have a proper look at it. But it was late and he was getting cold and, although he did not like to admit it, he was more than a little spooked by the way he had ended up here. . . .

Tomorrow, he decided. Tomorrow he would come back after school and have a look. It would still be dark, but there would be people around and he could bring a flashlight. He would know where he was and how to get home.

Arthur straightened up and let the branches of the bush spring back over the street name: Jursall Street.

CHAPTER 4

The next evening was wet and windy. The rain angled in through the broken upper windows of the old carpet ware-house that was the Cannoniers' den and spattered the floor. The wind stirred the dust and moaned around the iron roof supports and tattered remnants of carpet.

Flinch shivered. She was huddled into her coat, only her face visible peeping out. She liked the sound of the wind, it kept her company. But the rain was another matter. The bed of blankets and carpets where she curled up to sleep was in a well-sheltered place beneath an old staircase that led to the upper story of the warehouse. They never went up there—the floors were rotten and the steps were treacherous.

"So what do we do now?" Meg was asking. "Keep watch on the house and see who comes and goes?"

"People come," Art said thoughtfully, "but they don't seem to go. I have a strange feeling that even if Jonny had waited there all night, he would not have seen the figure come out again."

"Disappeared," Flinch breathed. "Like the woman we saw."

Art nodded. "I don't know what to make of it really."

"I think we should go and look," Jonny said. "Explore the house."

"It was spooky." Flinch didn't like the idea of going back.

Jonny shrugged. "You spooked the bats," he said. "The light you saw was probably a car."

"And the sound? The rumbling laughter?" Art reminded him.

"I don't know. But you were frightened, you said so yourself." Jonny grinned. "You don't usually turn tail and run, Art. We all know that."

"I ran," Flinch said. "I was scared."

"I was too," Art assured her. She was still holding his arm, and he pulled her slightly toward him. "I'd have been even more scared without you there, Flinch. It all sounds much less frightening when you talk about it. You're right, Jonny, we were spooked by finding the bats. Maybe the lights and the sounds wouldn't have worried us otherwise. Maybe they were just a car or something."

"The whole house shook," Flinch remembered.

"It looked about ready to fall down anyway," Jonny said.

"So what are you saying, Jonny?" Meg demanded. "That we should go back?"

"There's the mystery of the disappearing woman," Jonny told her. "We have to solve that."

"Do we?"

He looked startled, as if the question had not occurred to him. "Well, of course we do. We're the Invisible Detective."

"She was probably hiding upstairs."

"Won't take long to solve, then."

"I ain't going back in that house," Flinch said quietly.

"Nobody has to do anything they don't want to," Art told her. "But if Jonny thinks it would be a good idea to look around, then that's fine. I can't think what else to do, to be honest."

Meg stood up. "I'll go in with Jonny," she announced.

"I thought you weren't interested," Jonny said, surprised.

"Someone needs to stop you from tripping over your feet and hold your hand when the bats get you." She sounded serious, but there was a slight turn to her mouth and Flinch could see that Meg was joking—or as close as Meg ever came to joking.

Jonny stuck his tongue out at her. "Don't worry, Meg. I'll save you from the ghost soldier."

"We'll come too," Art decided. "But Flinch and I will keep watch outside. You can yell if you need saving from anything besides each other."

Art was amused to find that Flinch remained determined not to go back inside the house, even to unbolt the door for Jonny and Meg. Art and Meg between them were able to lever the board away from the window enough for Jonny to slip behind it and climb through.

While she was not prepared to do it herself, Flinch seemed happy enough to offer advice to Jonny as he disappeared into the darkness. "You need to put your hands out in front of you so you don't fall too far," she called after him. "And make sure you take the chair that isn't broken if you need to stand on it to reach the bolt."

She was frowning as she tried to think what else to tell him. Her expression relaxed at the muffled sound of a cry and a thump. "Oh, yes," she said. "Watch out for the little table by the door."

A minute later, Jonny opened the door. His face looked pale, but he forced a smile. "Thanks, Flinch. I'll be bruised for days."

"Sorry."

"Ignore him," Meg said, pushing into the hallway. "I'll make sure he doesn't fall over anything else."

Art grinned at Jonny. "Don't let her bully you. We'll keep watch from across the road. If a car comes, we'll make a note of the time. You do the same if you see strange lights and stuff."

"Good idea." Jonny glanced over his shoulder. "I'd better find her before she gets into trouble." He grinned at Flinch, brandishing his flashlight. "Don't worry, I'm fine. Look after Art." Then Jonny switched on the flashlight and gently closed the door, leaving them alone in the shadows of the porch.

The street remained deserted, so Art and Flinch did not bother to hide. They sat on the low remains of a wall on the opposite side of the road. It was at the end of a back garden, and overgrown with creepers and ivy that seemed determined to work their way into the old masonry and between the bricks. It had rained earlier and although it had stopped now, the bricks were still damp. Art lifted Flinch onto the wall before hauling himself up beside her.

There was nobody about, but they spoke in low voices. It was cold and dark, and their breath was a faint mist in the air before them. The house seemed to be staring back through its dark upper windows. A couple of times they thought they could see the faint light from Jonny's flashlight through the windows. But after a while there was nothing.

Then Flinch grabbed Art's arm and pointed. "Look," she gasped.

He could see it at once—a faint glow above the front door where part of a pane of glass designed to let light into the hallway remained. The intensity of the light seemed to vary, as if the source of it was changing. It was brighter than the flashlight's beam—brighter and more yellow. Moments later, Art could make out a glowing tinge around the edges of the board on the lower window. Light was escaping from where they had levered it away from the window frame. Art could imagine it creeping up the stairs, just as it had followed himself and Flinch the previous evening.

"The car must be on the road behind," Flinch said.

"That's no car," Art said quietly. "Listen."

There was a rumbling sound now. It seemed to come from the foundations of the house opposite them. Art could feel the wall beneath him trembling as if in fear. A tile on the roof of the house slid noisily across its fellows before falling to the ground and shattering with an explosive sound. Flinch jumped and gave a startled shriek.

Art put his arm around her. "It's all right. I don't know what it is, but it's all right."

"What about Meg and Jonny?"

"They'll be fine. I expect they'll be out in a minute, laughing and telling us what it was. Something very ordinary I expect."

Art did not really believe what he had just said. In fact, he hoped they would come out as frightened as he and Flinch had been. He hoped they would decide that some things were best left alone and that this was one of them. He hoped they would be out any second now. But the seconds turned to minutes and still there was no sign of them. The house was dark and silent again.

After perhaps ten more minutes, Art could stand it no more. "I'm going to check if they're all right," he told Flinch. "You wait here."

But she leaped down from the wall after him. "I'm coming with you."

"Sure?"

She nodded, eyes wide and face pale beneath the ingrained dirt and grime. Art could not pretend he wasn't grateful for the company as he turned the door handle and pushed the door hesitantly open.

Inside, the hallway was dark and empty. Art shone his

flashlight across the dusty floor. "Jonny?" he called in what was little more than a harsh whisper. "Meg?"

"Upstairs?" Flinch suggested.

"We'll check down here first. The last thing we want is to miss them. They could be waiting for us outside while we're looking for them in here." He thought of suggesting Flinch stay by the door in case Jonny and Meg appeared, but she was holding tightly on to his sleeve.

The downstairs rooms were all empty. It was weird going through them in exactly the same way as they had the previous night, but again they found nobody. They started tentatively up the stairs.

"Watch out for the bats," Flinch hissed.

"Don't worry, I remember."

He did not go into the room immediately at the top of the staircase this time and he switched his flashlight off. He stood at the door and called, "Are you in there? Jonny? Stop messing about, will you? Flinch is frightened." But while it was possible that Jonny might have hidden for a joke to spook them, Art could not believe that Meg would be so childish.

The other rooms were empty too. They had not been in them before, so it took longer to check them, as Art was not so sure of the geography. What he thought was a connecting door through from one bedroom to another turned out to be a wardrobe. He almost banged his nose on its back wall before stepping out sheepishly. Flinch had her hand over her mouth, covering her amusement.

"Maybe they went out the back door," Art said as they picked their way back down the stairs.

"It was jammed shut," Flinch reminded him.

There was only one door they had not tried, Art realized. The cupboard under the stairs. But that had been locked the previous night. He tried it anyway, giving the handle a good tug. And, to his surprise, the door opened easily. Art shone the flashlight inside, expecting to see a small cupboard with an angled ceiling. Instead the light showed them a steep flight of stone steps leading downward. There was a chill to the air, and a smell of damp and dust.

"A cellar," Flinch exclaimed.

"Well," Art said with relief, "that explains it. That woman must have gone down to the cellar. And that's where Jonny and Meg are. Maybe they've got stuck."

Or maybe they found some clues, Flinch thought, as they made their way down the steep stairs. There was no rail, so Art ran his hand down the wall as he went. The stairs were slightly damp and slippery. The whitewash on the walls was flaking under his fingertips.

The steps led down into a large room. The ceiling was vaulted, whitewashed brickwork and there were arched alcoves on all four sides of the room. Each alcove had a shelf at the back, like a seat built out from the wall. The floor was made of uneven flagstones.

Art shone the flashlight around the room and into every alcove. It was immediately clear that there was nowhere for anyone to hide, and equally clear that the room was empty. Flinch and Art just stood at the bottom of the stairs, watching the flashlight play over the flaking whitewash. For a full minute, neither of them spoke.

"What if they were down here when we were upstairs?" Flinch said eventually.

Art nodded. He had had the same thought. "They might be outside by now, waiting for us. There is another possibility," he told her. "We didn't actually look in the room with the bats."

Flinch drew in her breath sharply. "You think the bats got them?"

"Unlikely," Art reassured her. "But we'd better check. Just in case."

Flinch bit her lip and nodded. "Better check," she agreed.

Art forced a smile. "But I bet they're outside, wondering where we've got to."

He shone his flashlight cautiously into the room. He kept it angled on the floor, and wished he hadn't when it picked out the piles of bat droppings that were scattered across the bare boards. Slowly, carefully, Art moved the flashlight beam up the wall.

There did not seem to be as many bats as he remembered. Dark shapes clung to the shadows by the window. A line of bats was hanging from the curtain rail; the curtains themselves were shredded. Above them there was a hole in the ceiling and Art guessed that the bats came and went at night as they wanted.

"No Jonny or Meg," Flinch whispered. "You really think they're outside?"

Art did not answer. He stepped back out of the room and then froze in surprise.

They had both heard the sound from below—the sound of a door opening. From the galleried landing, Art could look down into the hall and see that the cellar door was swinging open and light was spilling out into the hallway.

"Thank goodness," he breathed, grinning at Flinch. He took her hand and was about to hurry down the stairs. But then a thought occurred to him and instead he crouched down, pulling Flinch with him, so they could peer cautiously through the banisters. "The cellar was empty," he whispered to Flinch, putting his finger to his lips.

She nodded and mirrored his action to show she had understood.

In the hall below, a figure stepped out from the cellar door. It was a man dressed in a dark coat. As Art watched, he reached up and put a top hat on his head. In his other hand he held a silver-topped cane. Art glanced at Flinch and saw that she too had seen.

The man started down the hall. But he paused before he got to the door and spoke in a loud, clear voice. For one terrible moment, Art thought he had seen him and was talking to them. "Everything seems to be back on track," he said.

"I'll be the judge of that, thank you, Lawson." The answering voice was shrill and reedy—a woman's voice. Art could see her now as she followed the man—Lawson—down the hall. Even from above and behind, he could tell it was the same woman he and Flinch had seen enter the house the night before, with her dark hair cut very short.

"I'm sorry, Miss Gibson," Lawson replied.

They were both waiting in the hall, waiting for a third figure that was closing the cellar door behind himself as he walked slowly along to join them. His head was down as he walked, so that all Art could make out was a mass of white hair.

"As it happens," the woman was saying, "I agree with your assessment. I think we can now proceed with the main plan." She turned to the white-haired man. "If your nephew is up to the task."

"I can assure you he is," the older man replied. "Though I must repeat that—"

"Please don't bother," the woman interrupted. "We are well aware of your views, just as we know how irrelevant they are."

The man in the top hat eased the door open and looked outside. "Thought I bolted it," he said, just loud enough for Art to hear.

He and Flinch edged back from the banisters.

"You're getting careless," Miss Gibson told him angrily. "Make doubly sure next time. We can't have people just wandering in. Again."

"Into a haunted house on a derelict street?" Lawson laughed. "Anyway, it's locked." He jiggled the key, and Art could imagine his surprise and worry at the fact that the door was not in fact locked.

"Just do as you're told. We can't be too careful. All clear?"

"Of course." Lawson was still looking puzzled as he held the door open for the woman. "Like I said, nobody ever comes here. That's why we chose it."

Miss Gibson stepped through the door. Lawson followed her, not waiting for the older man to leave. He followed them out, turning to close the door. As he did so, Art and Flinch both caught sight of his face. Both gave a gasp of astonishment. Art rose to his feet in surprise.

And the man looked up—straight at them. For a moment all three stood transfixed: Art and Flinch at the top of the stairs, Art looking over the banisters and Flinch through them. The man was framed in the doorway, staring up at them. The side of his face was illuminated by the light from outside. His pale eyes were wide with surprise. Then he pulled the door closed behind himself.

"Charlie?" Art gasped. He looked down at Flinch, who was every bit as surprised as he was. "What's Charlie doing here?"

There were posts at the end of the street, to stop cars from using it as a shortcut. The posts were old, crumbling concrete. One of them had moss growing up around its base. A cracked red reflector was set into the top of another where the other posts had empty sockets.

Arthur had come into Jursall Street from the opposite direction. Now that he knew where it was, that was the shortest route. He had run almost all the way from school, since it had to be quicker than waiting for the tube. The nearest station to Jursall Street was Borough and even that was quite a walk.

In the fading, graying light of the winter evening, the house looked just like what it was—a neglected, derelict, deserted house. Not a skull, not haunted, not even that spooky. The path was overgrown, the windows broken. The threatening glare it had fixed him with the previous night was bleached away by the last gasp of the sun sinking behind the lowest clouds.

There was nobody about. No one lived on Jursall Street anymore and Arthur now knew that it was a road to nowhere. Only people who were lost would have any reason to find it. It was probably simply a matter of time before the developers discovered the place and moved in. Then the crumbling stonework and broken glass would be replaced by red bricks over steel frames. What ghosts there were would move on. . . .

Arthur had intended to have only a quick look. Or so he had tried to convince himself. The flashlight he had in his coat pocket was there to find his way home again in the dark.

Who was he kidding? Without thinking about it, he had walked up the path, careful to avoid the brambles and the slippery moss on the flagstones. He tried the front door, without any real hope. Probably he would have to tumble through the window like Flinch and Jonny, all those years ago. . . .

But the door opened. It was stiff, creaking in protest from lack of oil on the ancient hinges, but it swung back. It jammed on the warped floorboards on the other side before it was half open, though there was ample room for Arthur to get through. He paused merely to glance over his shoulder at the darkening deserted street outside, then he was in the house, closing the door.

It was exactly as he had imagined from the Invisible Detective's casebook. It was exactly as he had dreamed about it. . . . He closed his eyes and tried to visualize the pencil floor plans sketched in the casebook. And he listened. He waited for a full minute, his ears straining to pick up the rumbling laughter of the house, of the ghosts. But there was nothing.

The rooms seemed not to have changed. The dining room was still a mess of broken furniture, with the one surviving chair now sagging and sorry for itself. Only the dust appeared to have survived the years unscathed. With every footstep, Arthur sent a powdery cloud into the air, until he was coughing and his cheeks were wet from his streaming eyes.

He was on his way upstairs, deliberately leaving the cellar till last, when he heard it. A chuckle of distant sound, almost metallic in its quality. Then the rumble that built till the whole house seemed to shake. Arthur felt a strange thrill at actually being there, actually experiencing it. He turned and ran down the stairs, feeling his foot sink into the rotting boards at one point but pulling it clear before he was trapped.

The door under the stairs had also rotted. A section of it was missing, the wooden upright having long since fallen away. And through the ragged gap that it left, Arthur saw the lights. Only faintly, of course. Just what light was escaping into the cellar. But again he could feel the excitement. He pulled the door open, the wood soft and damp under his hand.

He went slowly down the stone steps. They were slippery and worn. The sound and the light had faded into the distance now, and the flashlight provided his only illumination. Once at the bottom of the steps, he stood and swung the flashlight around the walls—just as Art had done. It was as if he was experiencing the same moment for a second time: déjà vu.

Which alcove was it? He tried to remember the plan, to

recall which way it was drawn. Now that the light had gone, he was unable to see the telltale cracks around the edge of the door. He knew he should remember. In his imagined memories of 1936, he had been through it so many times. . . .

The first alcove was solid. He thumped on the wall and was rewarded with only a dull thud and a whitened fist. There was a dark patch on the wall where the whitewash had fallen away at his touch. When he put his finger to it, gray powder trickled out like a tiny waterfall.

The second alcove also revealed no secrets. It was the third that surprised him. He leaned into it, not really expecting to hear a different sound from the wall. He was pretty sure it was the alcove directly opposite the bottom of the stairs that he was after. But as Arthur turned around and hammered on the wall, the flashlight angled so that he could see an iron ring set into the side wall. It had been painted white and had it not rusted so much it would have been practically invisible against the whitened bricks.

He was able to pry the ring away from the wall. His hand fitted neatly inside the cold, flaky metal. So, Arthur pulled.

There was a click and the back wall of the alcove swung slightly open. It seemed to be hinged so that the door would close on its own, and it soon swung gently back into place, clicking shut once more. So Arthur pulled again, and this time reached out and pushed the door, holding it open as he shone the flashlight inside.

It should have been disappointing. The area concealed

behind the wall was small. Possibly it was intended for storage—there were the remains of metal brackets on the back wall and a single wooden shelf was still in place. The others had fallen to the floor, together with some of the brackets.

But this was not what held Arthur's attention. This was not what made him gasp and step back, his hand to his mouth. The door swung slowly shut again, enlarging the circle of flashlight as it approached. It was just a glimpse that Arthur had through the closing door, but it was enough—enough to see that their clothes were faded, stained and tattered. Their hands and faces had long since decayed, leaving skeletal fingers and blank, staring skulls that shone white in the flashlight beam. . . .

Then the secret door clicked efficiently back into place, cutting off the sight of the two bodies lying on the floor behind it.

CHAPTER 5

Charlie was waiting for them outside. Art and Flinch spent a full five minutes summoning up the courage to make their way downstairs and out of the house. The key turned easily and quietly in the lock, which Art now realized was because it was well oiled and well used.

The street outside seemed as deserted as ever.

"Where's Meg and Jonny?" Flinch asked immediately, looking around.

"Maybe they're hiding. Waiting for those people to leave." But Art knew that as soon as they had seen him and Flinch come out of the house, they would have run across to them.

"You know, you're the last people I expected to find here," Charlie said. He had been standing quietly at the side of the house. Now he stepped out onto the path. Art could see that his expression was grave. He seemed somehow older today, drawn and tired.

"Hello, Charlie," Flinch said.

Charlie managed a smile at this. "Miss Flinch," he said, with a tip of his hat. Flinch giggled. "You're out late. I think it's time you were getting back to the den, don't you?"

"Is the house really haunted?" Flinch asked.

"Is that what you were doing? Looking for ghosts?" He started down the path, evidently expecting Art and Flinch to follow him.

"Sort of," Art said quickly. He nudged Flinch to be quiet. There was something wrong, something about Charlie's behavior that he did not like. "There was this old tramp, he said he'd seen a ghost here. A soldier."

In front of him, Charlie stopped suddenly. He turned slowly to face Art and Flinch. His face seemed even more pale now in the weak moonlight. "There are no ghosts here," he said, his voice little more than a hoarse whisper. "Nothing to interest you. Or the Invisible Detective. You understand?" His eyes seemed to flash with anger as they caught the light.

Art did not reply, he was too surprised at Charlie's tone. "You understand?" Charlie demanded again, and Art thought for a moment he was going to grab him by his arm. But then he seemed to sag slightly and forced a thin smile. "Just imagination and shadows. An old man's delusions."

Art nodded slowly. "Yes. That's what we thought."

"But then he turned up dead," Flinch said. "So there's a mystery."

Charlie seemed startled. "Dead? What—here?"

"No," Art said. "A mile or so away."

Charlie let out a long, misty breath. "There are no ghosts here, Art. No reason for you to be here at all. Is that understood?"

Art frowned. "What are you trying to say? Are you warning us off? Is that it?"

Charlie gave a short laugh and continued down the path, waiting for them on the pavement beyond the broken gate. "There's nothing to warn you about. Just an old house that's in danger of falling down. It could be dangerous to go inside. We were just surveying it. It may be condemned, torn down." He nodded, as if deciding this was a convincing story. "Best to keep away. All of you."

But Art was not convinced. Nor, it seemed, was Flinch. "Is it to do with your nephew, Charlie?" she asked with a frown. "Those people mentioned your nephew."

Charlie just stared at her. Art could see his mouth twitch and his eyes seemed more moist than usual. "My nephew is in the army," he said after a moment. "He's stationed miles away." Then, without further explanation, he turned and moved off briskly down the road. "Keep away from here, Art," he called as he went, without looking back. "Keep well away."

"What about Meg and Jonny?" Flinch asked again as Charlie disappeared into the night.

"He said 'all of you,'" Art replied thoughtfully. "Almost as if he knew Jonny and Meg were here too."

"You think he's seen them?" Flinch asked. "In the house? When they did their survey?"

"You don't survey houses at this time," Art told her gently. "You do it in daylight. And it isn't done by peers of the realm and women in posh suits."

"Then what . . ."

"They came up from the cellar. But we checked the cellar and it was empty. We went straight upstairs and yet somehow they were right behind us."

Flinch was watching Art closely. "What do we do, Art? Go back to the den?"

He shook his head. "No. We take another look at that cellar."

The cellar seemed as damp, dark and empty as before. Art swung the flashlight around, examining each of the alcoves in turn. But there seemed to be no doorway or opening they had missed.

"It must be hidden," he told Flinch. "But we know there's another room down here somewhere."

Flinch was darting in and out of each of the alcoves, having a quick look before moving on to the next one. "This it?" she called out.

"What?" Art hurried to see what she had found. It was a small ring embedded in the side wall. "Pull it and see what happens," he suggested.

Gleefully, Flinch pulled the ring out from the wall, and Art could see that it was attached to a thin chain that fed into a hole in the brickwork. As she pulled it, there was a dull click from the back of the alcove. A section of the wall swung open—a concealed door.

"I was right," Art said. He grabbed the door to stop it from immediately swinging shut again and pulled it fully open, scarcely daring to think what might lie beyond. . . .

Flinch and Art both stared in disappointment at the large cupboard they had found. The small room was about four feet deep and the back wall had half a dozen wooden shelves on it, supported by metal brackets. On the shelves there were several paint pots, a screwdriver, jars of nails and nuts and bolts.

"I don't think they would have hidden in here," Art decided.

"No Jonny or Meg either," Flinch said in a flat voice.

"There must be another hidden door," Art said, allowing this one to click shut again. "Has to be."

"Where?" Flinch wondered. She crossed to another cubicle, examining the side wall for more metal rings.

Art returned to the steps. He stood at the bottom and shone his flashlight down at the floor. Sure enough there was a trail of damp and dusty footprints. But they were now crisscrossed with his own trail and Flinch's frantic rushing about between alcoves. It was difficult to make out the other sets. "Wish I'd thought of that before," he muttered.

It looked as if there might be a line of footprints into the alcove directly opposite the stairs. He followed it with the flashlight. But in the alcove itself there was no trace. Which was odd, Art decided. Flinch's prints were obvious in the other alcoves, and he had watched her rush in and out of this one. So why . . .

Because the floor was clean, he realized as he stepped into the alcove. There was no dust. At least, there was no dust on the floor, just several areas of sprinkled whitewash. But the "shelf" where the wall stuck out at the back was thick with dust. Art shone the flashlight down to examine the dust—and there it was.

"Flinch!" he called in an excited whisper. "Look here."

In the dust on the whitewashed bricks someone had scrawled two letters, tracing them with their finger probably. J and M. For Jonny and Meg. And beside the letters was a simple arrow that pointed to the back of the shelf.

"What does the arrow mean?" Flinch asked.

Art knew she could not read, but she probably knew the initial letters of their names by sight.

"I'm not sure." He pushed at the brick immediately above the arrow, but nothing happened. So he tried the next one up. Again, nothing.

The fourth brick shifted under Art's tentative finger. He felt it give slightly, so he pushed harder, using the heel of his hand. The brick slid smoothly into the wall and, with a scraping sound, the whole of the side wall of the alcove moved aside.

"A secret passage," Flinch gasped, staring into the blackness beyond.

But before Art could comment, they again heard the rumbling sound that had frightened them before. It seemed closer now, as if it was coming from the blackness of the passage. It grew in volume and the whole floor started to shake beneath their feet. Flecks of whitewash fell through the flashlight beam and sprinkled the floor.

Flinch gave a yelp of astonishment and fear, and hid behind Art.

Then the light came. A faint glow that moved along the passage from its distant end. Art could see that the passage sloped downward. The light grew brighter as it rushed along it toward them. It was a line of broken flashes—light, then brief darkness rushing along the walls until it spilled out into the cellar and up the steps. Even with the wall closed, Art could imagine enough light escaping into the cellar to be visible in the hallway above—just as they had seen it the night before.

"It's like a train going past," Flinch shouted above the noise, staring anxiously up at Art as the light flashed across their faces.

"Yes," he agreed. "I think you're right." He grinned at her as the light faded and the noise began to subside. "And I bet I know where this passage leads. Come on."

As Art had surmised, the passageway ended at a station platform.

Flinch looked around in surprise. "The underground? But . . . it isn't a proper station, is it?"

The walls were bare—no advertisements or maps. There was not much light apart from the flashlight. The platform was narrow, with a white line painted along the edge. There was a smell of fuel oil in the air.

"I think it's a sort of service area rather than a station," Art decided. He shone the flashlight along the platform.

What other light there was came from an archway further along the platform. Art lowered his voice to a whisper. "Let's see what else is down here."

The archway led directly into an open space with other archways branching off. Art could hear the sounds of machinery and people talking and laughing. The whole area was better lit, so Art turned off his flashlight. He and Flinch both stepped back onto the platform as a man in a white coat appeared from one arched doorway and walked across to another.

When the man had gone, Art slipped out from hiding and, with Flinch close on his heels, scurried across to see where the man had come from. There was no door in the archway and they could see right into a large room beyond. Careful not to be spotted, they stood to the side of the arch and peered carefully around.

"What is it?" Flinch hissed.

Art shrugged. He did not know. "Looks like a hospital," he murmured back.

The room was big, square and well lit by lamps that hung on metal poles from the vaulted ceiling. In the middle of the room was a large table. The end was angled, so that the figure lying on the table was slightly raised and seemed to be looking back at the entrance. Except that the figure was unconscious, a heavy dark mask held over its face by a white-coated man.

Beside the table another man, again in a white coat,

was measuring out black rubber tubing. He took a knife from his coat pocket and cut off a length of the thin hose.

"What are they doing?" Flinch wanted to know.

Art put his finger to his lips and shrugged.

The man with the knife and the tube was standing with his back to them now, obscuring their view of the table. Art was aware of a rhythmic pumping sound, and when the man moved, he could see what looked like a small set of bellows expanding and contracting. They seemed to be attached to the figure on the table. He stared fascinated as the man moved aside again. He was no longer holding the hose.

"I'm going to look for Meg and Jonny," Flinch whispered in Art's ear.

He nodded, not really taking in what she had said. His attention was on the table, on the figure.

"Just need to check the connections," the man was saying. "Then we're all done with this one. Right, let's have him on his feet, shall we?"

The other man removed the mask from the figure's face. Then he put his hands beneath the figure's shoulders and levered it upright. Art gasped and drew back instinctively. He glanced around for Flinch, but she had disappeared.

The figure on the table was sitting with its legs over the edge now and the first man pulled it to a standing position. The man, if it was a man, was wearing a khaki uniform—an army uniform. Art could see now that the table had not been angled at all. The reason the figure's head and shoulders had been slightly raised was because it was wearing a backpack. But it was not this that had made Art gasp in fear and surprise. It was the figure's face—revealed when the mask was removed.

It was the face of a huge rat. Except that somehow there was an almost human quality to it as well. It was covered in stubbly short hair. A snout rather than a nose protruded from the face, over a narrow lipless jaw from which broken, yellowed teeth jutted prominently. The eyes were deep-set and fiercely red. Yet despite the hair, the whole face seemed drawn and drained. Like a rat's skull.

Art could also see now that the creature—for it was obviously not a man—was attached to the bellows machine by another of the black tubes. As he watched, one of the white-coated men turned the creature sideways and opened the backpack. It was hinged at the base and the front swung down to reveal a mass of machinery. Art could see what looked like a small gas cylinder, a miniature version of the bellows and a large dark box that seemed to be leaking oil and looked like a car battery. With the back open, he could hear a quieter version of the rhythmic "breathing" of the bellows like a faint echo.

The two men examined the contents of the backpack for several moments. One of them made adjustments and then pulled out the pipe that was attached to the large bellows machine. The other man closed the backpack up again. They both stood back to regard their work.

"Excellent," one of them said, just loud enough for Art to hear. "Put him with the others. We'll take five minutes, then get started on the next one." He turned toward the entrance where Art was hiding.

Art stepped back, out of sight, and looked around for Flinch. He had no idea what was happening here, but he didn't like it. It was time to get out, time to go for help. Except there was no sign of Flinch. He could sense the two men approaching the archway. He could hear the rhythmic mechanical breathing of the rat creature as it followed them.

A hand touched his shoulder and Art whirled around. He stifled a cry as he saw it was Flinch. She had her finger to her lips, mirroring his earlier gesture, and beckoned for him to follow.

There was a narrow corridor along the side of the room he had been looking into. Art had not noticed it, but Flinch evidently knew where she was going as she led him quickly along it. They passed several metal doors with grilles set into them at eye level. But the grilles were covered over with metal shutters and he could not see inside.

"Where are we going?"

"They're just along here," Flinch whispered in reply. "I couldn't undo the bolts."

She stopped at last in front of a metal door. This one had heavy bolts drawn across at the top and bottom, but the shutter was open. Through it, Art could see Jonny and Meg, their faces pressed up close as they waited for Flinch to return.

"Thank goodness," Jonny said as he saw Art.

"About time," Meg told him.

The bolts were heavy and stiff but, by working them up and down, Art was eventually able to pull them back. The door was hinged inward, so Jonny and Meg had to step back as Art opened the door. But neither of them made any attempt to leave the room.

Jonny looked as if he had seen a ghost. Art glanced around for Flinch, but again she seemed to have disappeared. Instead, the woman in the suit—Miss Gibson—was standing there. Beside her was Lawson, the man in the heavy coat. He was not wearing his top hat and Art could see that his hair was dark and thinning and greasy. Instead of his silver-topped cane, he was holding a revolver and it was pointed at Art.

"If you had told me the door was unlocked straight away, it might have saved an awful lot of bother," Miss Gibson said to the man.

Art did not move, he just stared. But it was not the woman he was staring at. Nor was it the revolver. It wasn't even that he was wondering where Flinch had gone. He was looking at the third figure, the older man standing calmly and quietly in the background.

Charlie stepped forward, so that he was standing between Miss Gibson and Lawson and directly in front of Art. "I warned you to stay away," he said softly. "But you just can't leave things alone, can you?"

Arthur was amazed how much noise and light there was. Especially the light. It burned around the edges of the side wall of the central alcove, illuminating the cellar so that every flake of whitewash was harshly visible. The whole cellar shook as the train rumbled past close behind the wall.

He stood in wonder as the light played over him. Then, as suddenly as it had started, the light show finished. The sound of the train rumbled on into the distance, eventually fading back into the silence of the cellar. Arthur was left alone again in the semidarkness. But now he knew where the hidden door to the unused station service area was. And he had seen something else too—something he had missed as he shone the flashlight into the alcoves.

Resting on a shelf of bricks at the back of the central area, positioned perfectly in the middle as if it had been left there deliberately for him to find, was a clock. He examined it carefully with the flashlight before picking it up. It was a brass carriage clock, dulled by a coating of dust, and it had stopped at ten minutes past seven.

Arthur picked up the clock and brushed the dust from its face. It was surprisingly heavy for its size—it fitted easily in his hand. As he shone the flashlight onto the dial, he could see that there was writing across the clockface. A maker's name, perhaps. He angled the flashlight so he could read the stylized script more easily.

Edax Rerum

It seemed familiar. A phrase he had *seen* somewhere before, though he could not remember where. A crossword clue maybe? An anagram? Axe Murder, he thought suddenly, and almost put the clock down. But he was being daft, he decided. Surely nobody would put an anagram of Axe Murder on the front of a clock.

As he considered, he turned the clock over, looking for a key to wind it up. Maybe it would still work. There was a key, folded down so that it did not protrude from the back of the clock. Arthur wiped the side of his hand across the back of the clock to clear the film of dust. As he did so, he could see that there was something written on the back as well. Above the key. Engraved.

Or rather, there had been. Two words, it looked like, but they had been scored out. Someone had taken something sharp, like a thin-bladed knife, and scratched them out. The marks were deep, determined and, by the angle, hurried and careless. Another mystery.

If he held the flashlight to the side, he could make out some of the original letters beneath the scratches. The engraving had been in the same stylized script as the two words on the dial. Two words here as well. The first began with an *M*, the second with a *W*—the capitals were easier to read.

Before he knew it, Arthur was sitting on the shelf of bricks where he had found the clock, staring intently at the letters as he tried to make them out. Without really thinking, he lifted the head of the key and turned it. It moved easily, the mechanism within clicking efficiently as he wound the clock. It started to tick with a satisfying rhythm, and Arthur turned the clock back over to set the hands.

The clock now said half past six. But a minute ago it had been ten past seven. Quarter past six. Six o'clock . . . The thing was broken after all—the hands were moving backward. As he watched, they spun ever faster until the movement was a blur. Arthur shook his head and turned the clock over again, once more examining the letters scored out on the back.

The second word seemed to say "Wall." There were several other letters after that. The first word might be "regret," though there was an *M* at the front of it. . . .

Arthur was still staring intently at the back of the clock when he heard the ghosts.

"I'm not convinced by Lord Fotherington's commitment to the project," a woman's voice said clearly.

Arthur almost dropped the clock.

She was standing at the bottom of the stairs, a middle-aged woman smartly dressed in a dark linen suit, her dark hair cut very short. Beside her was a man in an overcoat. He was putting on a top hat and held a silver-topped cane.

"Too concerned about his nephew, if you ask me," the man said. "What if he doesn't give us the endorsement?"

They were starting up the stairs, seemingly without noticing Arthur in the alcove behind them. Arthur suddenly realized that he could see through the two people—he could clearly see the steps in front of them. Their feet were insubstantial as they moved up the stone staircase. He could see the door at the top was closed, yet the woman made the gesture of opening it. And she did open the door. But it was also still closed, only a shadow of it swinging open.

"I think we shall have to do something about dear 'Uncle Charlie,' " she said in a mocking tone as the two of them stepped out into the hallway.

The ghost of a door swung shut behind them and they were gone.

Arthur felt the clock slipping from his hand and fumbled to keep hold of it. It had stopped again, he saw, though he could hear it ticking. As he juggled the flashlight and the clock, the light shone across the scored-out letters on the back and, with a moment of sudden clarity, Arthur could see that they had once said *Margaret Wallace.*

CHAPTER 6

Behind Miss Gibson, Lawson and Charlie, Art saw a door opening. Flinch stepped quietly out into the corridor behind them. She looked at Art, obviously at a loss for what to do.

But Miss Gibson had seen Art's attention shift and she turned to look—immediately catching sight of Flinch. Lawson had also turned, though Charlie still had Art fixed with a steely gaze.

Without thinking, Art launched himself across the corridor, straight at the three adults. His shoulder connected with Lawson's hand, sending the gun flying. It skidded away, coming to rest further down the corridor. Off balance, Lawson fell. Charlie also fell, although Art had barely touched him. As he lost his balance, the older man grabbed at Miss Gibson's jacket, as if trying to save himself, and she too landed heavily on the floor.

"Run!" Art yelled. He struggled to pull away from the tangled mass of flailing arms and legs, but someone was holding on to his arm—Lawson. Behind him he could see Meg emerging from the cell and coming over to help him.

"Leave me," Art told her, struggling desperately to wrench his arm away from Lawson's grasp.

If the others tried to help, they would all be caught. Miss Gibson was shouting for assistance and it could only be seconds before someone heard her.

"We mustn't let them get away," Charlie shouted, his voice almost as loud as Miss Gibson's.

Meg's eyes widened at Charlie's voice and she seemed about to say something. But Jonny bundled her ahead of him and the two of them ran down the corridor after Flinch, who was already at the far end. But still Art could not break free.

Charlie was pulling himself to his feet and grabbed Art, breaking Lawson's hold as he did so. "Not so fast, young man," he snarled with an anger that Art had never seen in him before. But his grip was weaker than Lawson's and Art easily pulled himself free. He turned to run after Jonny and the others.

Miss Gibson, however, was standing directly in front of him—holding the gun.

They hid in the darkness on the other side of the street. The moon was obscured by thick clouds and mist hung in the air around them.

"What now?" Jonny wanted to know. "What about Art?"

Meg hissed at him to be quiet. "I don't know," she said. "I just don't know. We need to think about this."

"What's Charlie doing with those people?" Flinch asked. "Will he help?"

"Maybe." That was something else Meg needed to think through. "What would Art do?" she wondered out loud.

"He'd go to the rescue," Flinch said without hesitation. And she was right.

"That man had a gun," Jonny pointed out. "And there were those . . . things." He looked around nervously. "Will they let him go?"

"I didn't get the impression they were going to let us go," Meg said.

"We should go back," Flinch decided.

"They'll be waiting for us," Jonny said.

"We're just kids," Meg replied. "They'll expect us to run away and hide. And we're not doing that. Flinch is right. We must get Art out."

Jonny looked as if he was going to say something, but before he did, there was a sound from the house opposite. They all turned to look—in time to see the front door open and a dark shape emerge. It was one of the misshapen ghost soldiers. He was followed by another before the door shut. They stood on either side of the porch, like sentries.

"We're not getting back in that way," Jonny said. "If there was just one of them we could distract him, lead him off, but not two."

"Around the back?" Meg wondered.

"Locked solid," Flinch told her.

"Of course, it isn't actually the house we need to get into."

"What do you mean, Jonny?"

He shrugged. "Maybe we could get a train. Get out at that station."

"It's not a proper station," Flinch said. "The trains didn't stop there."

"They didn't even slow down, so we couldn't jump out. Even if we could time it right and get the doors open."

"Must be on the Northern Line," Jonny said. "Some sort of service area. Maybe for post . . . Doesn't the Royal Mail have its own tube system or something? Mail Rail?"

"There is a way . . . ," Meg said slowly. "It's a bit risky, though. What's the nearest station do you think, Jonny?"

"Borough."

"What are we going to do, Meg?" Flinch's eyes were shining in the faint glow from the misted streetlamp at the end of the road.

"We go to Borough," Meg decided. "Hide on the platform when the station closes and the trains stop running."

"That'll be a couple of hours yet," Jonny pointed out. "They run till nearly midnight, I think."

"Then what?"

"Then we walk through the tunnel, back to that service area or whatever it is, rescue Art and walk out again."

"Avoiding the live rail?" Jonny asked. "And any staff who are still around? And that woman and the man with the gun and the ghost soldiers or whatever they are?"

Meg nodded. She was not happy with the idea, but she could think of nothing else. "We can't just leave Art there."

Jonny shook his head. "And I thought you were the sensible one."

. . .

Art sat alone on the floor of the small locked room for what seemed like hours. He could hear the occasional rumble of trains outside. They did not seem very frequent—as if they were off on a spur of some sort from the main underground system.

The floor was hard and cold, but there was no chair in the room. The light came from a single naked bulb suspended high up near the ceiling. The only things that broke the monotony of the plain brick walls were the door and, in the opposite wall, a grille through which came a draft of stale, humid air.

At first he had thought he could pry the grille from the wall and crawl out though the shaft beyond. But it was too high up for him to reach—on tiptoes, his fingers just grazed the bottom of the mesh—and it looked too small.

Sometimes there was the sound of footsteps from the corridor outside. Art always tensed as he heard them, assuming that whoever it was would be coming to see him. But always the sound faded into the distance and the door remained firmly locked.

Until, eventually, after he had decided that he was just being left there to rot, he heard the sound of several people approaching. This time, the door was unlocked and opened. Outside in the corridor stood Lawson, once more holding the pistol. With him was Charlie, looking as severe and angry as Art had ever seen him.

"Leave me with him, Lawson," Charlie said. "I'll get some sense out of the brat."

Lawson considered this. "All right. Just shout if you need me."

"He won't give me any trouble—will you, young man?"

Art did not reply.

"Now, then," Charlie said as Lawson stepped back into the corridor and swung the door shut, "I want to know who you are and what you're doing here. And I advise you to cooperate if you ever want to see the light of day again." He advanced menacingly on Art.

The bolts scraped home on the other side of the door and at once Charlie's demeanor changed. His face relaxed and he shook his head.

"You young fool," he said quietly. "Why didn't you keep away, like I told you?" He seemed disappointed rather than angry now. "I warned you what would happen, didn't I? I told you they wouldn't hesitate to kill you if they found you down here."

Art was confused. "You said to keep away," he admitted. "But you didn't say they'd lock us up. . . . Or kill us."

"In the cellar—I told you when I saw you in the cellar."

"But you didn't see me—"

Charlie was not listening to Art's protests. "It's too late now anyway. What's done is done. I just don't understand—"

This time Art cut Charlie off. "No," he said loudly, "I don't understand. You might have warned us off, but you haven't explained why you're so anxious we should keep away. You haven't told us anything. In fact, you helped get us locked up."

Charlie blinked, surprised at Art's outrage. "I tried to help you escape," he insisted. "I knocked away the gun, held back Lawson and Miss Gibson. And you still couldn't manage it. I told you," he said again. "In the cellar."

Art was ready to have another go at Charlie. "I thought you were our friend," he started. But the sound of the bolts drawing back stopped him.

The door opened once more and Lawson stood there, smiling with grim satisfaction. "It seems Miss Gibson was right," he said. "You do know these children."

"Don't be ridiculous," Charlie said.

"I was listening," Lawson snapped back. Then he slammed the door shut and shot the bolts across once more. His voice came through the small opening in the door as he said, "Miss Gibson will talk to you later," then added, in a mocking tone, "your lordship, sir."

Charlie closed his eyes and rubbed his face with his hand. "You see what you've done, Art?" he said quietly.

"How do I know that wasn't staged?" Art demanded. "How do I know he didn't pretend to lock you up so I'd talk to you, tell you what you want to know." But he was less sure of himself now. Charlie seemed so certain, so convinced they had spoken. It was hardly something he would lie about—Art would know the truth.

Charlie's eyes were watery in the harsh light. "The only

thing I want to know is why you didn't listen. Have you any idea of the sort of trouble we're in?"

They waited for half an hour after the last train had left Borough. They knew it was the last train, as a uniformed official—a porter or guard—hustled the passengers who got off it out of the station. Perhaps he was in a hurry to get home to bed, Flinch thought.

The three of them hid at the end of the platform, pressed into an alcove where a map of the tube system hung. After the guard had left, Jonny traced the Northern Line with his finger, tapping the point where he thought the service area might be.

"I'm just worried that it isn't on the main line," he said. "We didn't see and hear that many trains while we were down there, did we?"

"If they're doing something secret, they'd want somewhere more private," Meg agreed.

"Like a siding?" Flinch asked.

"A sort of branch line. Maybe a route back to wherever they store trains when they've finished for the day, or divert them if the main track's busy."

"Which way?" Meg wanted to know.

Jonny pointed to the tunnel mouth beside them. "Same way as the trains go. This is the northbound line." He jumped down from the platform. "Just keep well away from this rail with the insulators under it. They may turn it off at night, but I wouldn't want to bet on it."

Meg jumped down after him, turning to help Flinch. "And what if a train comes?"

Jonny grinned. His nervousness seemed to be gone and he was obviously enjoying the adventure. "Then I hope you like traveling with your back to the engine," he said.

Jonny and Meg both had flashlights, but the tunnel was so dark, they seemed to cast hardly any light. Flinch followed close behind Meg, staring down at the ground and keeping as far from the electric rail Jonny had pointed out as she could. The pale ceramic insulators were like upturned teacups and seemed to glow in the dim light, illuminating the path for a short way ahead into the darkness.

They walked slowly, carefully and almost silently for what seemed like miles. Jonny thought he had found a side tunnel at one point. But it turned out to be a deep archway with a huge junction box on the wall, cables emerging from it like thick tentacles. There was an almost bitter smell to the tunnels—soot and oil and what Jonny said was the "electric smell" mingled and clung at the back of Flinch's throat. She did not like it.

"Are we nearly there yet?" she asked, for about the fourth time.

And just as patiently as she had on each of the other occasions, Meg replied, "We really don't know, Flinch. But I hope so."

Jonny heard her too this time. "We don't know if this line even leads to the service area," he admitted. "But if it does we should be there soon, I think."

"And if not?"

"We'll end up at London Bridge station and have to wait there till it opens in the morning."

In fact, they almost missed it completely. Flinch was walking head down and stumbled. She grabbed for Meg's coat, catching hold and almost pulling the older girl over.

"Careful," Meg warned.

"Sorry."

But as Meg straightened up, catching her balance, the light from her flashlight glinted on the rails ahead—and on a set of points where the rails split. One track led straight on, while the other curved sharply to the right and disappeared into the darkness.

Jonny had seen it too as he turned to check if they were all right. He and Meg both shone their flashlights along the other set of rails, illuminating a narrow tunnel that led away into the distance.

"This could be it," Jonny said, his voice a harsh whisper. "It really could."

Flinch gave a yelp of excitement.

"If it is," Meg warned, "we need to be quiet."

"They won't be expecting us. Not through the tunnels," Flinch said. She was feeling excited now rather than bored. And proud too of how they had fooled the enemy.

It was not far along the side tunnel before they saw the service area ahead. The light filtered through the arches that led to the rooms and corridors behind it. They could hear activity as well—the sounds of metal being worked and of people talking and moving about. When they reached the short platform, they stopped, staying just inside the tunnel and out of immediate sight.

"What now?" Meg wondered.

"Maybe we should fetch Art's dad?" Jonny said. "This is getting serious."

Meg nodded. "I thought of that. But at the first sign of the police, goodness knows what they'd do to Art. We have to rescue him and get away from here before we go to the police."

"That might be tricky," Jonny said. "Look, you two wait here while I have a look around and see what's going on."

"Why you?" Meg asked.

"Because I'm quickest." And, as if to prove it, Jonny was gone.

He returned in less than a minute. "I don't like it," he whispered as he joined them again in the tunnel. "There are lots more people about now. And those soldier things too."

"They work more at night," Meg said thoughtfully.

"So how do we get Art?"

Jonny sucked in his cheeks. "I don't know. There are a couple of those skull-faced soldiers at the end of the corridor where they had us locked up."

"Assuming he's in the same place," Meg pointed out.

Flinch leaned out of the tunnel, straining to see. She did not like the idea of meeting a skull-faced ghost soldier, but equally she was not ready to abandon Art.

"What about the other end of the corridor?" Meg was asking.

"No idea where that is and we'd never get to it. The corridor runs parallel to the tunnel here, so we can't get to the other end without going through their base."

"Was there like a grille in the wall?" Flinch asked suddenly. She had seen something above the platform that gave her an idea.

"I don't know," Jonny admitted.

"I think so," Meg said. "Why?"

"There was one in the other room, where I hid," Flinch told them. "And there's one up there above the platform. Look."

Flinch could just reach the mesh grille when Jonny lifted her up on his shoulders. It came away from the wall surprisingly easily to reveal a dark metal conduit behind.

"I'm not sure I like this," Meg said from below. "What are you going to do?"

"Find Art," Flinch told her. "This runs along the corridor, so I can crawl through till I find the room where they're keeping him."

"It does look as if it goes along between this platform and then the tunnel and the corridor on the other side," Jonny said. "For ventilation, I suppose."

Meg folded her arms, watching as Flinch heaved herself up into the small, dark opening. "Why does Flinch have to go?"

"I don't mind."

"Because she's used to climbing about and stuff," Jonny insisted. "Anyway, she's in there now. I couldn't climb in, and I doubt I could lift you up there."

"I won't be long," Flinch told them.

"All right," Meg said. "Flinch, if you can't find Art, see if you can find Charlie."

"Can we trust him?" Jonny asked.

"I think so," Meg said. "You remember when he shouted that they mustn't let us get away?"

"Not offhand. I was a bit busy, as I recall."

"I heard him clearly," Meg told them. "I was watching his face as he said it."

"So?"

"So he was lying." Meg looked up at Flinch. "If you can't find Art, find Charlie. And if you don't find either of them, just come back and we'll think of something else. All right?"

Flinch nodded, then she twisted herself around in the narrow opening and started down the tunnel.

The metal surrounding the opening soon gave way to a brick-lined passageway. It was smaller once she was through the opening—there was only just enough room to inch along. She had hoped she could crawl on her hands and knees, but it was too low for that and she had to wriggle along on her stomach. She kept her arms stretched out in front of her and pulled. It was difficult while trying to hold Jonny's flashlight, but she was grateful for the light.

After a short distance, however, she realized that there

was light shining up into the tunnel through other small grilles. She paused and switched off the flashlight. Yes, there was just enough light to see the tunnel ahead. She managed to work the flashlight back under her body and tuck it into her blouse, wriggling it around until it was comfortably lodged at her side.

She made quicker progress without the flashlight, able to grip the floor of the tunnel properly with both hands and drag her weight forward little by little. But it was painful, the skin rubbing from her palms and fingertips, and she felt bruised all down her front. By digging her toes in, she discovered she could lift her body slightly so it was less painful.

Another reason for turning off the flashlight, Flinch soon realized, was that the light from it might be seen shining through the grilles she passed. Most of the rooms were empty as she peered through the mesh coverings. But occasionally she passed by a room where people were working—two white-coated men writing notes at a bare wooden table in one; a disheveled-looking man standing motionless in another, his features pinched and his eyes deep-set and shadowed. Flinch shivered and moved on.

The next grille she looked through gave into a larger room. There were several people in it. The nearest figure had its back to her and was wearing one of the large packs that the ghost soldiers wore. On the other side of the room Lawson stood talking to the smartly dressed woman, Miss Gibson.

They were speaking quietly, but their voices carried and Flinch could make out a few words and the odd phrase. She struggled to hear more, pressing her ear to the grille and feeling the cold, sharp mesh against her cheek.

As she pressed closer, the grille gave slightly, the top becoming detached with a sharp snap. It was so close to Flinch's ear, it sounded like a gunshot. She froze, terrified that Miss Gibson or Lawson had heard, but they were still talking. It was the figure closest to the grille, closest to Flinch, that reacted.

Slowly it turned toward her. Flinch shrank away, pressing herself against the back wall of the small tunnel, terrified that her pale face would still be visible through the grille.

The figure's face was drawn, almost white, bleached like bone. The skin, if it had skin, was tight over the skull, and the red eyes were so far back in their sockets that they were almost in shadow. They seemed to glow as the ratlike face loomed close. The bottom half of it was covered in rough stubble, the elongated jaw opening slightly with a hissing sound. A thin trickle of saliva escaped from a corner of the mouth, as if from a hungry wolf. A bony hand with long, tapering, stained fingers reached up toward the grille.

Without waiting to find out if the creature had seen her, Flinch heaved herself forward. She could feel the flashlight digging into her side, but she didn't care. She just had to get as far away as possible. Behind her she could hear a scraping, scratching sound, as if the long fingers were stroking the mesh.

For how long she struggled on, Flinch had no idea. It seemed as if she had been in the tunnel all her life. At any moment, she thought, she might get stuck and be trapped there forever. Was it just her imagination or was the tunnel actually getting smaller? Should she go back–could she go back? There was no way she could turn around and she had not tried to push herself backward. Part of her wanted to try it, to be sure she could retrace her journey, and another part of her was afraid to, in case she couldn't.

She was almost in tears as she looked through the next grille, expecting yet again to see a small empty room below her. But instead she saw two figures sitting cross-legged on the floor, staring silently at each other.

Art and Charlie.

With a laugh of relief, Flinch pushed at the grille with all her might. It fell away, clattering noisily to the floor, making both Art and Charlie jump with surprise.

"Flinch!" Art exclaimed, reaching up to the grille to catch her as she tumbled forward into his arms. He pulled her out, her legs trailing painfully across the bricks for a moment before they both collapsed laughing in a heap on the floor.

Charlie reached down and helped her up. "Miss Flinch, this is a surprise, I must say."

He reached down again to help Art. Art looked up at the old man for a moment, before accepting Charlie's hand.

"It's all right," Flinch told him. "Charlie's on our side–Meg said so."

Art's eyes narrowed as he looked again at Charlie.

"Art knows that," Charlie said quietly. "We've both had a rather busy day and that never helps one to think straight."

"How did you get here?" Art asked. "Where are Jonny and Meg?"

"They're on the platform outside. We came through the underground."

Charlie gave a short laugh. "Did you, by Jove?"

"I've come to rescue you," Flinch proclaimed proudly.

"That's very kind of you," Charlie said. But he did not sound as excited about it as Flinch had expected. "There is just one problem, though . . ." He looked at Art, and Art met and held his gaze.

"You see, we're locked in," Art said. "And while you might have been able to get to us . . ." He turned to look up at the hole where the grille had fallen away. Flinch and Charlie both looked up at it with him. "I'm afraid there's just no way that either Charlie or I will ever fit through that gap. We're still just as trapped as we were five minutes ago."

The cellar lit up once more as another train went through the service area beneath it. The sound and light jolted Arthur. He had no idea how long he had been staring at the back of the clock, his mind in a fog.

He turned the clock over, but of course the time it said bore no relation to reality. Between quarter and twenty past eleven. It was still ticking, but the hands did not seem to move. He felt around the back until he found the key, then turned it, still watching the clockface. Sure enough, the hands started to move backward again. Useless. He was tempted just to leave it here, except for the name on the back. And something else. Something about clocks, possibly this clock, that he could barely recall. Something he had read. . . .

Of course! There was something about clocks in the Invisible Detective's casebook. He could remember reading it. He could remember the faded ink, the rough sketch of a clockface in the margin beside Art's handwriting . . . his own handwriting. He could almost feel the rough texture of the old notebook. But he could not remember a word of what he had read.

The hands of the clock were slowing now, as if they had tired of the rapid movement. And again a voice startled him.

"I almost didn't see you there."

Arthur gasped and stood up, clutching the clock and the flashlight to his body. The light from the flashlight was lost in his coat.

"No, stay in the shadows, you never know when someone might come." The man had come silently down the steps and now he stepped into the cellar. He was smartly dressed

of the locked door? Footsteps coming across the room as someone came to investigate who had tried to open the door? Someone or something . . .

Before he knew it, Arthur was running back along the landing, down the stairs two at a time. One gave way beneath him and he pitched forward, just managing to catch the banister rail and haul himself upright again.

The door was opening. He could hear the scraping turn of the key, the click of the lock, the squeal of the hinges. Arthur pulled his foot free of the rotting wood and raced down the last few stairs. His head was ringing, echoing with the sound of his own heartbeat in time with his feet on the bare wooden boards of the hall, the sound of the front door as he opened it and ran out into the cold night beyond.

The air outside was crisp and fresh. Arthur was running, trying to put as much distance as possible between himself and the house as quickly as he could. His head was still echoing with the sound from upstairs. The sound of a voice. The sound of a voice that had called down the stairs after him.

"Arthur? Is that you, Arthur Drake?"

CHAPTER 7

"Things have got out of hand," Charlie admitted.

The three of them—Art, Charlie and Flinch—were sitting on the floor just inside the cell door. Flinch looked downcast. Art had suggested she return to Jonny and Meg, but she seemed loath to repeat her journey along the airshafts. Art's mind was working through all the possibilities he could think of. Charlie was explaining what was happening.

"I was supposed to be monitoring the experiment—providing a reasoned, impartial appraisal." He shook his head. "I should have called a halt to it as soon as I learned what Miss Gibson was really doing."

"And what is she doing?" Art wanted to know. "What are these 'ghost soldiers' exactly?"

"Spooky," Flinch offered. "That's what they are." She shivered and folded her arms tightly around her chest.

"They are certainly that," Charlie agreed. "Originally, Miss Gibson and Dr. Lawson asked for government funding to research a group of people who had come to our attention. Biological research. Medical research, they said at first. You see, these people . . ." He paused, thinking for a few moments before he went on. "Well, they're different from you and me. Not through any fault of their own. But under certain circumstances they, well, change. No one really knows why or how, or even what causes it."

"What do you mean, change?"

"It's a subtle thing. Not like a werewolf, though I've heard that comparison made. The teeth lengthen, the jaw protrudes, the fingernails and toenails are elongated. . . . Enough to be measurable, even noticeable."

"The ghost soldiers?" Flinch gasped.

Charlie nodded.

"But that's a huge change," Art said. "It's more than noticeable."

"Yes," Charlie said sadly. "And that's thanks to Miss Gibson and Dr. Lawson. At first they said they wanted to observe and analyze the changes. Find out what causes them, decide if there is any danger. But then they started to . . . interfere."

"You mean they're making these people change?"

"I'm afraid so. And more than that. They have exaggerated the metamorphosis. They've used drugs and treatments to make it more pronounced. That was when they came back to the government for more funding. Only this time it was not for research but for development."

"Developing what?"

"You called them 'ghost soldiers' and that's really what they have become. Miss Gibson is creating an army. Not only have they increased the changes, but they have altered the nature of that change. You see, the original creatures in the experiment were friendly—animals rather than monsters, if you like. They were still, up to a point, human, though they certainly didn't look it. In fact, they were more like giant rodents."

"Ratty," Flinch said suddenly.

"What's that?"

"Ratty," Flinch said again. "I've seen that man before, the one with the cane. He was talking to Fredericks about Ratty."

"The creature in the sewers." Art shuddered. "The Shadow Beast."

"Of course," Charlie said, his face clearing. "I did hear that you had found the missing specimen. In fact, they have lost several."

"But the ghost soldiers we saw are nothing like that," Art said.

"No. Their next step was to create creatures that were more aggressive, instinctive. No longer even human in temperament and emotion. Violent and dangerous, bred to fight. And, worse than that, they are no longer using the poor patients they originally identified. Now they can turn anyone into one of these creatures. Anyone they think won't be missed or is not important." He shook his head sadly. "Human beings."

"That's awful," Art murmured. "People . . . anyone. Just taken off the streets." He glanced at Flinch and tried not to think about it.

Charlie got to his feet and went over to the door. He stood for a while, looking out through the small hatch into the corridor beyond. "But even that wasn't enough for Miss Gibson. Now they are adding mechanical 'enhancements,' as they call them." He turned back to face Art and

Flinch, his face drawn and pale. "The limbs are strengthened with a metal exoskeleton, while nutrients and fluid are fed into the bloodstream so they don't have to stop to eat or even sleep." He sighed. "It's an abomination."

"They're making monsters?" Flinch asked.

Art nodded. "They certainly are."

"And they're making them out of people." Charlie put his hands over his face for a moment. "And I have let them."

"Why?" Flinch asked.

"Flinch!" Art hissed. He could see that Charlie was upset.

"No, it is a fair question. Why?" Charlie sat down next to them again. "The plan is that Miss Gibson will create a regiment of these ghost soldiers. A fighting elite that could just make all the difference if and when war comes. Troops that can work tirelessly behind enemy lines and on what we call special operations. They won't need resupplying and they will never get tired or scared or give up. Other soldiers won't have to work alongside them, as they are self-sufficient. The whole thing can be kept secret, but if there are rumors, then that will simply add to the fear they strike into the enemy. Just having such a regiment is worth the huge cost."

"Human cost?" Art wondered quietly. "So that's why you've gone along with it—sacrifice a few people to save the many."

"I wish it was that calculated and defensible," Charlie

said sadly. "No, you can indeed make an argument along those lines. It might have been my opinion if I had been consulted at the start of all this." He fixed his pale eyes on Art. "But whatever I might have thought, they have gone too far. I know that now, despite the fact that they have tried so hard to conceal their real work from me. The cost of what they are doing can never be repaid. But they are almost finished. There's just one final test to convince the War Office."

"What's that?" Flinch wanted to know.

"An exercise. An exercise against a regular army unit. Or rather, a unit of crack troops. If the ghost soldiers acquit themselves well, Miss Gibson will get the go-ahead for mass production." He sighed and shook his head. "Mass production," he muttered. "Using innocent people. . . ."

"But if you're in charge of monitoring all this, can't you just stop the exercise?" Art asked. "Why not call a halt now?"

Charlie turned away. His voice was quiet and strained. "Because I don't know when or where the exercise will take place. And because the officer in charge of the special army unit the ghost soldiers are exercising against is Captain Algernon Maltravers." When he turned back, Art could see the glistening trail where a single tear had run down one of Charlie's cheeks. "He's my nephew. And Miss Gibson has made it very clear that if I speak out against her project, Algie will suffer an accident during that exercise. Or even before it. A fatal accident."

There was silence for a while. "We'd better warn him, then," Flinch said at last. "Before you stop these people."

Charlie smiled thinly. "Yes, Flinch. I think you're right. Warn Algie and then stop the experiment." He nodded slowly. "That's what I should have done long ago. You make it sound so simple. . . . Unfortunately, we can't warn anybody or stop anything while we're locked up."

"Yes, I've been thinking about that." Art grinned. "And I think it's time we got out of here."

The brickwork was hard and cold against Flinch's back. She was pressed against the wall beside the door into the cell. Next to her, Art was hammering on the door with his fists and yelling at the top of his voice. Charlie was lying on the floor of the cell, his eyes closed.

It was several minutes before anyone came. Flinch could not see who it was from where she was standing. But Art stopped hammering and spoke loudly and nervously.

"He just collapsed. I think it's his heart. He mentioned he has some tablets in his coat, but I don't know where that is."

There was some muttering from the other side of the door. Then Art glanced over at Flinch and winked.

"One of the scientists. He's gone to get someone. Lawson or Miss Gibson, I expect." He smiled at her. "Don't worry—it will work."

Flinch nodded in reply. But she was not sure. "I could just slip out," she said. "Hide, then open the door for you."

"That would be easier," Art agreed. "But you couldn't manage the bolts before."

It was only a minute before they heard urgent footsteps along the corridor. The bolts drew back and the door was flung open. Flinch stopped it with the palms of her hands, slowly pushing it away slightly from herself. Through the crack between the door and its frame, where the hinges were, she could just see Lawson standing inside the doorway. He was holding the gun and looking suspiciously into the room where Art was kneeling beside Charlie.

"Well, help me," Art said urgently. "Can't you see he's ill?"

"It's a trick," Lawson said. But he did not sound certain. Flinch was tempted to slam the door in his face. She did not like Lawson.

"Move away from him," Lawson gestured to Art with the revolver. "Back over there."

Art stood up and stepped away from Charlie's prone form. "Take a look," he said.

Lawson stepped slowly into the room, tracking Art with the gun. Flinch could see him on the other side of the door now, stooping carefully beside Charlie. She pushed the door slightly further away and stepped out from behind it. Lawson was alone, which was a relief. She had been worried he would bring one of the rat men with him.

As Lawson crouched down beside Charlie, feeling over his chest while at the same time trying to watch Art and keep the gun leveled, Flinch ran at him. He was just starting to straighten up, starting to say something, when Flinch's hard little shoulder rammed into the small of his back. Lawson stumbled forward, tripping over Charlie's body.

He cried out in surprise and alarm. Then in anger as Charlie was suddenly moving, reaching up and grabbing the gun from his hand. Charlie's feet kicked upward, helping to propel Lawson across the cell. He landed on his back, his head cracking on the hard floor. For several seconds, Lawson seemed to be struggling to stand up. Charlie had the gun now and was pointing it at him. But then Lawson fell back with a groan, his eyelids fluttering and his head slumped to one side.

"Well done, Flinch." Art ran over and gave her a hug.

Charlie was checking Lawson. "Out cold. Yes, very well done, young lady."

"Should we tie him up?" Flinch wondered.

"No, he'll be out for a while," Charlie said. "We'll just lock him in."

"Now all we have to do is find Jonny and Meg," Art said.

Finding them was easy. Getting to them was not. Charlie led the way, saying that since most people had seen him with Miss Gibson and Lawson he could probably bluff his way out. But while they passed several occupied rooms, no one saw them as they made their way quietly back to the station area.

Once they arrived, it was a different matter. There were several of the ghost soldiers standing in a line on the platform, between the arched opening where Art and the others emerged and the tunnel where Flinch said Meg and Jonny were hiding. And with them were a scientist in a white coat holding a clipboard and Miss Gibson. There was no way they could get past to join Jonny and Meg.

Art could hear Miss Gibson's shrill voice as she spoke to the scientist. "It may be for the best," she was saying. "But I think under the circumstances we shall have to bring our schedule forward. I've told Dr. Lawson and he agrees. How soon can your team have sufficient specimens ready to fight?"

The scientist went through notes on his clipboard. His voice was quieter and Art could not hear him. But he could see something moving at the mouth of the tunnel beyond. A head was poking out into the dim light as someone else strained to hear what was being said.

Flinch had seen it too. "It's Jonny," she said.

Art put his finger to his lips. "We can't get to the tunnel while they're there," he whispered.

"Through the house, then," Charlie replied quietly. "If we keep close to the wall, we shall be in the shadows."

Art agreed. They could probably make the short journey to the cellar entrance without being seen. But he did not like to leave Jonny and Meg waiting for them down here. "We've got to tell them somehow."

"Wave?" Flinch suggested.

Actually, Art thought, that was not a bad idea. Miss Gibson and the scientist had turned away while they examined the notes on the clipboard. The ghost soldiers were standing absolutely still, at attention. Worth the risk, he decided. He gestured for Flinch and Charlie to stay put, then stepped out onto the platform, into the light. He could see Jonny's face, pale against the dark tunnel behind. Hoping Jonny had seen him, Art waved and pointed to the other end of the platform.

But Miss Gibson was turning back toward them now. "Monday, then," she was saying. The scientist started to speak, but she dismissed the comment with a quick gesture. "You've voiced your concern about their lack of discipline and restraint before. But that isn't what we're demonstrating, is it?"

Her heels echoed off the platform as she walked toward the archway—toward where Art and the others were hiding. Behind her, Art could see Jonny bob up for a moment to wave back at him—he had seen them. But Art was more worried that Miss Gibson was about to see them herself. He turned to retreat into the open foyer on the other side of the arch, but a group of the ghost soldiers was lining up here as well.

"Run for it?" Flinch asked quietly. Her eyes were wide with anticipation and fear.

But at that moment, Miss Gibson stopped. She turned back toward the scientist and called, "If some of the soldiers do get killed, that will prove everything we have said." She was standing between the archway and the scientist—obscuring his view, Art hoped. "Even Lord Fotherington won't be able to stop us then."

Pushing Flinch ahead of him and gesturing urgently for Charlie to follow, Art ran quickly and lightly along the platform, keeping close to the wall. They reached the other end, ducking into the shadows, just as Miss Gibson turned back and continued on her way to the arch where they had just been hiding.

Art breathed a sigh of relief. "Now for the easy bit," he said.

But, in fact, the easy bit lasted only as far as the hallway. As soon as they emerged from the cellar through the door under the stairs, Art could see that one of the ghost soldiers was standing on guard by the front door.

Luckily, it was standing at the foot of the stairs rather than in the middle of the hall, facing the door. There was no way they could leave by the front door, that was obvious. But they might be able to sneak into the front room. And from there it was just possible that they could get out of the same window that Flinch had come in through.

They tiptoed along the hall, expecting that at any moment the figure by the door would turn its ghastly face toward them. There was a rifle slung over the thing's shoulder and Art watched the tip of the barrel anxiously for any sign of movement.

But there was none. It could have been a statue, and the

three of them managed to get into the front room without being seen or heard.

Flinch led them over to the window. She pushed the board away from the frame, making a hole large enough to climb through. Large enough for her and possibly for Art—after all, Jonny had managed to get in. But there was obviously not enough room for Charlie. Art helped Flinch widen the gap, but as soon as they pushed the board further from the frame, the nails that held it in place began to shriek and protest. They stopped quickly.

"If it hears us, will it come in?" Art asked Charlie quietly.

He nodded. "I expect so. They'll just obey orders. But if it's guarding the door, it has enough initiative and reason to listen out for intruders."

"We can't leave Charlie here," Flinch said.

"I agree. They'll find we've escaped before long. Then they'll start searching." Art turned to Charlie. "Any ideas?"

Charlie was smiling, his teeth as white as his shock of hair in the dim light. "Just one," he said. "Flinch, have you ever played Knock Down Ginger?"

They helped Flinch out through the gap between window and board, then moved quietly back to the door and positioned themselves so they could see the ghost soldier in the hall.

Art was counting in his head. Sure enough, when he got to twenty, there was a loud knock at the door.

Immediately, the ghost soldier seemed to come to life.

The rifle was off its shoulder in an instant, held in one hand as it turned the key, pulled back the bolt and opened the door quickly.

There was nobody there. For a moment the figure stood framed in the doorway. From its silhouette it could have been an ordinary soldier. Then it turned slightly, teeth and snout now visible. The joints of the metal frame that encased its legs and arms hissed and whirred as it stepped out onto the porch, swinging the rifle in a low arc as it searched for a target. Still nothing.

"A bit further," Art breathed. "Just a bit further."

The ghost soldier took another step forward, down the first step into the garden.

Art and Charlie moved silently to the front door. They were only a few feet behind the creature. If it turned now, it would see them. The rifle continued to pan across the garden. Another step. Then it stopped.

Art glanced at Charlie and mimed pushing the ghost soldier, but Charlie shook his head. His fearful expression suggested this was not a good idea.

The soldier was turning, back toward the house. Another second and it would see them.

"I often used to wonder what happened to Algie." Arthur's grandad reached carefully into the desk drawer and lifted out a photo album. He gestured for Arthur to sit beside him as he opened it. The cover had a design of interwoven flowers, scratched and faded. The photographs inside were sepia-toned and brittle with age. Grandad turned the pages slowly and carefully, as if he was afraid they might crack, like some of the photos.

"Ah, here we are." Grandad stopped turning the pages.

The photos were held in place by large black photo corners that clipped their white borders, fixing them to the thick gray cartridge paper. Where the glue had perished, some corners fell from the pages as he turned them. A good number of the photographs had slipped sideways where the photo corners were gone.

Grandad repositioned the photograph at the top of the page, smoothing it gently with the side of his wrinkled hand. Like the other pictures, it was a faded brown. The once-white border was mottled and the image it showed was slightly out of focus.

"This was after the fire, of course. Taken by the police photographer."

The picture showed a park, with four figures standing on the grass. Behind them clouds of smoke drifted across. Blackened struts stuck out of the ground like blighted trees and there was a blur of uniformed people standing watching.

But Arthur's attention was focused on the figures—the children. "That's you, isn't it?" he said, pointing to the taller of the two boys.

He had not realized quite how alike he and his young

grandfather looked. He recognized the serious set of the face despite the satisfied smile. He knew the dark eyes and the curl of unruly hair above his right eye. Arthur could see why Charlie had thought that he was Art.

Next to Art was Jonny—looking taller than he was because he was so thin. He was grinning nervously, his sepia-black hair pushed back from his high forehead so that his ears seemed to stick out. Arthur smiled at that.

Flinch was instantly recognizable. In the photograph it was impossible to tell how grubby she must have been. Her long fair hair was hanging over her shoulders and her wide smile seemed to reach right across her face.

Then there was Meg. She was standing slightly behind the others, as if wanting to be apart from them. Her arms were folded and her face was set in a stern, almost sulky expression. Her head was tilted slightly to one side, so that the mass of curls that Arthur knew had been a brilliant auburn fell away. But despite her solemn look, despite the fuzziness of the picture, there was something about her eyes that suggested it was all a pretense, an act—and that beneath the veneer she was grinning like the others, happy to be with her friends.

Grandad was smiling too. His face seemed the younger for it, and for a moment Arthur could see himself in about sixty years. . . . And that was somehow both uplifting and terribly sad at the same time.

Slowly, perhaps sadly, Grandad closed the book. "*Tempus edax rerum,*" he murmured.

Arthur blinked. "What?"

Grandad shook his head. "Nothing. It was a long time ago. A long, long time."

"Did you say 'edax rerum'?"

The old man nodded. "What of it?"

"I've seen it written," Arthur explained. "Recently."

Grandad's mouth twitched. It did that when he was suppressing a smile. "On a clock, perhaps?" he asked quietly.

"What does it mean?"

"Tempus edax rerum," Grandad said again. He got stiffly to his feet and replaced the album in the drawer before he answered. "It's Latin," he said as he turned to face Arthur. "It means 'Time devours everything.' " He glanced down at his hands, curled as if he was still holding the photograph album. "And you can take it from me, it's true."

He sat down again, in the small armchair this time, facing Arthur. "Where was the clock?" he asked. "In the antiques shop?"

"No. I found it."

"Ah. And where is it now?"

"I left it in a haunted house," Arthur said, forcing a laugh—trying to make light of it. But he had an idea the question was more serious than it sounded.

Grandad nodded. "Just as I did," he said.

CHAPTER 8

Just as the ghost soldier started to turn, a shower of gravel scattered across the porch. Art saw several of the small stones bounce off the creature's snout, and, with a snarl of anger and surprise, it turned back toward the garden and started down the path.

At once, Art and Charlie followed it down the steps. At the bottom they dived back into the narrow gap along the side of the house, pressing themselves into the shadows. Art could see the soldier halfway down the path. It had stopped, its head lifted as if it was listening, or perhaps sniffing for the scent of its prey. Art held his breath. How long would it stay there? Had it seen—or smelled—Flinch?

Eventually, the soldier turned around and came back along the path. A hiss of steam escaped from the joints of one knee. It disappeared from sight, into the porch, and Art heard the front door slam shut.

He could hear Charlie breathing heavily beside him. "Come on," said Art, and they both ran to where Flinch was waiting for them on the other side of the road. As they reached her, she grinned and dropped a handful of gravel.

Jonny had been worried that they would be trapped in the locked-up Borough station and have to wait for it to open in the morning. But when he and Meg crept back along the tunnel, they could see light and hear the sound of laughter.

They peered cautiously around the end of the tunnel and saw that there were people on the platform. Several women were sweeping dust off the platform into dustpans. They had their hair tied up in scarves, probably to keep the dust out of it. A man in a guard's uniform was holding open a trash bag and another woman was dropping a hand-ful of rubbish into it—a paper bag, chocolate wrappers, a discarded newspaper . . .

"Looks like we're stuck here for a while," Jonny whis-pered to Meg.

In fact they were there for only a few minutes before the guard tied the top of the bag with a piece of string and shouted, "All right, ladies. That'll do for tonight. Time for breakfast."

"You get your own breakfast," one of the women quipped as they filed past him and off the platform. The sound of their laughter and conversation became a low mumble in the distance.

"Come on," Meg said. "Let's follow them out."

"What?" But Jonny recognized the tone of her voice, and anyway she was already climbing up onto the plat-form and hurrying after the women.

There were other cleaners appearing from the depths of the station and even from the other tunnel. They seemed to be moving slowly, and Jonny could see as he and Meg joined the dozen or so cleaners that the escalators were not operating, so they had to walk up what was in effect a steep staircase. Jonny was relieved to notice a couple of young children—all less than ten, probably—among the group. He and Meg drew some puzzled looks, but nobody commented.

There was a heavy iron gate across the station entrance. The guard they had seen had pulled it partway open and was standing beside it. He said good-bye to everyone, calling some by name, while others got just a nod and a grunt. He frowned as Jonny and Meg approached, and put his arm out to stop them.

"What're you doing here?" he said, his voice gruff and stern. "You're not fluffers."

"Yes, we are," Meg told him indignantly.

The guard was not convinced and continued to regard them suspiciously. There were mutterings from the women waiting behind them. Jonny heard someone say, "I ain't never seen 'em before. You, Mildred?"

"We came with my auntie," Jonny said quickly. He pointed vaguely across the street to where a couple of the women were disappearing into the distance. One of them happened to glance back for a second. "There she is," Jonny went on quickly. "Please, she'll be cross."

The guard grunted, still frowning. But he moved his arm and let them through. "You tell her to check with me before she brings kids in here next time," he called after them. "You tell her . . ."

They discussed whether to look for Art and the others back at the haunted house or go to the Cannoniers' den.

Jonny was not keen to return to the house, so he was relieved that Meg also thought the den was a better idea.

"I doubt they'll want to hang around there unless they have to," she said. "I wouldn't. But if they aren't at the den, we'll try the house. In case they need rescuing."

"Again."

Art and Flinch were already at the den. Art was sitting on a roll of carpet, hunched over his casebook and scribbling furiously. Flinch was curled up in her makeshift bed of carpet remnants and old clothes, fast asleep.

"You took your time," Art said without looking up.

"What a cheek!" Meg exclaimed. "It was you who needed rescuing."

He did look up now, grinning with evident relief that they were back safe. "Ah, but you two needed rescuing first, didn't you?"

Meg did not reply. She flopped down on the carpet next to Art, who made an exaggerated joke of coughing at the flurry of dust this produced.

"Where's Charlie?" Jonny asked.

His voice was loud with nerves and Flinch stirred in her bed. She yawned and stretched, and in a moment was wide awake. "Jonny!" She leaped up and hugged him tightly.

"Careful," he told her, "you'll crush me."

But Flinch had seen Meg and ran to embrace her too.

Art watched with amusement. "I'm pleased to see you

as well," he said. "And in answer to your question, Charlie went home."

"He didn't say good-bye," Flinch said, disappointed.

"He did," Art assured her, "but you were already asleep. Anyway, I've got a lot to tell you about what's been happening. But Charlie's gone to put a stop to it all."

"As easy as that?" Meg wondered.

"Well, he has to talk to his nephew, who's in charge of some special army unit on an exercise. Only we don't know where that exercise is taking place. So it is a bit tricky. He's got to contact the War Office and try to find out where Algie—his nephew—is based."

Flinch was looking at Art openmouthed. "Could he be at Dartmoor?" she asked.

"Why Dartmoor?" Art asked her. "I mean, I suppose it's possible. . . ."

"Is there somewhere on Dartmoor called Princesstown?"

"I'm pretty sure there's a Princetown," Jonny said. "Isn't that where the prison is?"

"That's where Algie is, then," Flinch said firmly.

"How do you know?" Meg asked her.

" 'Cause I heard that Gibson woman say so. When I was crawling through the tunnels, she was talking to Lawson. She said the army was ready at Princesstown—"

"Princetown," Jonny corrected her.

"And the exercise would be at Dartmoor."

"That must be it," Art said, clapping his hands together. "Well done, Flinch."

Flinch grinned with delight, the grin turning into a huge yawn.

"Oh, don't," Jonny protested. "You're making me feel tired."

"I think we're all tired," Meg observed. "It'll be dawn soon. I want to get home and try to sneak in before anyone else gets up."

"Yes, good idea. Maybe they'll think we've been there all night."

"Dad's working, so I won't be missed," Art told them. "You all get some sleep while you can, and we'll meet back here tomorrow afternoon." Art yawned too. "Oh, I'm glad it's Saturday, so there's no school."

Meg folded her arms. "What are you going to do?"

"I'm going to tell Charlie where his nephew is. With any luck, this will all be over by the time I see you again, and on Monday the Invisible Detective can report another case successfully closed."

Charlie was on the telephone when Art arrived at his house. It was a large residence, with a long gravel driveway. Charlie was actually Lord Fotherington, and his butler, Weathers, let Art into the house and ushered him through to the drawing room.

Charlie waved at Art and motioned him to a seat. He

listened at the phone for another minute, then hung up with a curt farewell.

"Nothing," he confessed to Art. "Either nobody who's in the office at this time of night knows anything or they won't say."

"Algie's at Princetown," Art said simply. "Flinch overheard Miss Gibson speaking to Lawson. She says the exercise is at Dartmoor."

Charlie regarded Art carefully for several seconds without replying.

"Does that make sense?" Art asked, wondering if Flinch had got it wrong.

"Yes, a lot of sense. You know, you Cannoniers never cease to amaze me." Charlie raised his voice and shouted, "Weathers."

Immediately the butler was at the door. "Sir?"

"I know it's early, but we're famished. Do you think you could arrange breakfast?"

"I'm sure that's possible, sir," Weathers replied with no hint of irritation. "We may have to resort to yesterday's bread, as I'm afraid the baker has not yet called."

"I'm sure we'll manage."

Charlie was on the phone again by the time Weathers had closed the door. Art leaned back in the chair and closed his eyes. He was so tired. As if from a great distance, he could hear Charlie saying, "Summerfield? Yes, Fotherington here again. I want the number for Princetown barracks, if you could find it for me. . . . No, I want it now. I'll wait."

But that was the last Art heard as he drifted into a sleep where an old man sat alone in a small room leafing through an old photograph album.

The clatter of a tray being set down on the coffee table in front of him woke Art. He had no idea how long he had slept and he still felt incredibly tired. But he rubbed the sleep from his eyes, mumbled a thank-you to Weathers and stared in sudden hunger at the plate of eggs, bacon, fried bread and mushrooms that rested on the tray. He could smell the strong coffee.

Charlie was sitting opposite him, already cutting into his bacon. "Just finished speaking to Algie," he said between mouthfuls. He looked much calmer, younger even, which Art put down to the fact he had spoken to his nephew and presumably warned him of the dangers he faced.

"He was a little skeptical at first," Charlie said with a wry chuckle. "But I think he's in the picture now."

"So what's happening?" The coffee was incredibly hot and Art set down his cup to let it cool while he turned his attention to the eggs and fried bread.

"Algie can only take his orders from the War Office, of course. So I need to get on to them pretty sharpish and have them confirm what I've told him."

"Which is?"

"That he and his unit should report back to London immediately. I've given him the location of Miss Gibson's base, and told Algie to go and round them all up. If we use his team, that keeps the number of people who know to a minimum, which will please the high-ups. The fewer faces with egg on them the better," he added, regarding a forkful of his own egg with amusement.

"So, it's all over?" Art felt relieved. He almost sank into the chair and faded back into sleep.

"Bar the shouting," Charlie confirmed. "It's nearly seven o'clock. As soon as I've finished my breakfast, I'll rouse Sir Robert. He owes me a couple of favors." He raised his steaming coffee cup as if in salute. "Here's to another case successfully concluded by the Cannoniers, on behalf of the mysterious Invisible Detective." He took a sip of the coffee. "I do look forward to one day actually meeting Mr. Brandon Lake, you know."

Art smiled. He was tempted to confess that there was no such person as Brandon Lake. But the Invisible Detective was the secret of the Cannoniers. No matter how good a friend Charlie might be, this was something special— something that Art, Jonny, Meg and Flinch kept to themselves.

"Right." Charlie set down his cup and rose to his feet. He licked his lips in appreciation of the breakfast he had just finished. "Now, let's get this settled." He crossed to the table where the telephone stood and reached out for it.

But his hand never got there. He never made the call.

The doorbell rang. Charlie hesitated, frowned. "Who can that be?"

Art did not hear Weathers open the door, but he did hear the man's startled shout. A moment later the door of the drawing room burst open. Framed in the doorway was one of the ghost soldiers. It paused, looking around, and seemed to sniff the air. Then it saw Charlie and gave a guttural roar of satisfaction.

The creature started across the room, joints hissing and jaw trembling with anticipation. It did not seem to notice the coffee table in the way and sent it crashing to one side.

Charlie backed away. There was another of the creatures in the room now, following the first. Art leaped up from his chair and ran to defend Charlie. He grabbed the knife from his plate, feeling the handle slippery with grease from the bacon and eggs. But as he ran at the first of the ghost soldiers, the second one swiped a massive metallic hand down through the air with a whirr. It crashed into Art's arm, sending the knife clattering away.

The first of them had reached Charlie now, its snapping metal-gloved fingers reaching for the old man's throat. Art was off balance from the blow, and before he could recover, the second ghost soldier lashed out again. It was closer to him now and the force of its attack sent Art flying back across the room.

He landed in the chair where he had just been sitting. It rocked under the impact and began to topple over backward. He cried out, his view of Charlie obscured as the ceiling did a somersault over his head. He bounced off the chair as it fell over and saw the floor rushing up toward him, saw the coffee table upside down on the floor. The leg of the table rocketed toward Art's face and he desperately twisted, trying to avoid hitting it. There was a sudden, jarring shock to his forehead that seemed to reverberate right through his whole body.

Then the world went black.

The way Dad explained things, he made it sound as if it was all Arthur's doing. He implied that Arthur was always talking about Sarah and how they spent time together at school. He never actually said it, but he certainly gave the impression that Arthur and Sarah being such good friends was what had prompted him to give Sarah's mum a call.

Maybe that was the reason, Arthur thought. But there was no need to go on about it. Especially as Sarah's mum—Linda—didn't seem that worried anyway.

What made it worse was that Sarah could obviously see how embarrassed Arthur was about the whole thing. She kept giving him little knowing smiles across the dinner table. Arthur had decided before they came that he would speak when he was spoken to, and then as little as possible.

This turned out to be easy. They arrived late and Sarah's mum already had the Sunday lunch ready to serve. Once seated, she and Arthur's dad did almost all the talking. Their repeated descriptions of how good it was to see each other again after all this time and how they really should make an effort to keep in touch, being such near neighbors and what with Sarah and Arthur being such good friends and everything, were punctuated by a steady stream of nonsense from Sarah's brother, Paul.

Paul was seven, with a round face and freckles. His hair was almost as black as Sarah's, but whereas hers was long and straight, his was a close-cut mass of dark curls. There seemed to be things stuck in it, but Arthur did not look too closely. Judging by the way the child wielded a fork that was far too big for him, it was probably breakfast.

"Do you see anything of Jeff these days?" Sarah's mum asked, slightly hesitant.

"That's my dad," Paul said to no one in particular. "I see him every other weekend. Unless there's football."

"Not since . . ." Arthur's dad paused to take a mouthful of lunch. "This is very good, Linda."

"She spent all morning peeling the carrots," Paul explained.

"No, not for ages. Not since I saw you both at the Johnsons', remember?"

"Was I there?" Paul asked.

"You were a baby," his mother told him. "Now eat your carrots, since you know how long they took to peel."

"They'll help you see in the dark," Arthur's father said.

Paul spiked a slice of carrot on his fork and held it up to examine. "It's got no batteries," he said dubiously.

Sarah's mum sighed. "Just eat it."

Sarah was giving Arthur one of those half smiles again. He wasn't sure if he was supposed to smile back. But then he realized that somehow he was already doing it. He turned his attention to his own carrots, staring down at his plate and wondering again what he was doing here.

"Mum says you're a policeman," Paul suddenly said to Arthur's dad.

Arthur looked up. His father seemed amused by the comment. "That's right," he said. "Actually, I'm a detective."

Paul looked at him, then at his sister. Then he looked back at Arthur's dad. "You're not invisible, are you?" he said.

There was silence for a moment, then Dad laughed. "No, I'm afraid I'm not. And you don't need to eat your carrots to see that."

"But—" Paul started to say.

"Paul," Sarah snapped at him. It was the first time she had spoken since they'd started eating. "You talk too much."

She was looking at Arthur as she spoke. And now she was not smiling.

CHAPTER 9

It was almost six o'clock and it was dark outside. Jonny had been at the den since four, Meg since soon after that. Flinch had been there all day. It was dull and wet and cold, so she had not been tempted outside.

By five o'clock Jonny had been anxious and fidgeting. Meg told him not to be daft and that Art would be there soon. They had not, after all, agreed on a specific time to meet and he would have got to bed later than the rest of them. But by six o'clock even Meg was visibly worried. She was biting at her bottom lip in a way that Flinch knew meant she was nervous but did not want to admit it.

"Maybe we should go and look for him," Jonny suggested. He had made the same suggestion several times in the last hour.

But this time Meg nodded without making a sarcastic comment. "Yes, maybe we should."

They both looked at Flinch. But before she could tell them that she thought Art would be there any minute, that he would never let them down, they all heard the sound of the back door slamming shut. Moments later, Art ran in.

He looked tired and drawn, and there was a large bruise on his forehead. "Thank goodness you're here," he gasped.

"We're here?" Meg said. "Where have you been? And whatever's happened to you? Come and sit down." She ushered him to a roll of frayed carpet, ignoring Art's attempts to push her away and his protestations that he was fine.

Art rubbed his face with his hands before looking up at their expectant faces. "Are you all all right?" he asked.

"We're fine," Jonny told him. "But what about you?"

"Did you see Charlie?" Flinch asked. She was desperate to know what had happened. "Is he sorting things out?"

"I saw Charlie," Art said. "And you were right about Dartmoor, Flinch. He phoned the barracks and spoke to his nephew, Algie."

"Thank goodness for that," Jonny said, and flopped down on another roll of carpet. He waved his hand at the cloud of dust that shot up.

"Yes, well, I'm afraid it isn't good news at all." Art's expression was grave as he looked around at his friends. Flinch felt suddenly cold. "The ghost soldiers came. To Charlie's house."

"What happened?" Meg demanded.

"I'm not sure. I only came to about an hour ago. Weathers is phoning the War Office, trying to persuade them that Charlie wants the special army unit brought back from Dartmoor to deal with the ghost soldiers. But even if he manages, it will take a long time for troops to get here. Maybe too long."

Flinch was listening carefully. There was something that Art had not said, something that was worrying her even more than what he had said. "Charlie. You haven't mentioned Charlie."

"Yes, what's happened to him?" Jonny wanted to know.

"He's not . . ." Meg's voice tailed off, and she put her hand quickly to her mouth as if to stop herself from saying any more.

"When I woke up," Art said slowly, "Weathers was already conscious. He got knocked out too, when they came in. He was dabbing my face with cold water." Art rubbed gently at his bruised forehead as he spoke. "The place was a mess—broken furniture, the front door still standing open. But Charlie . . ." He paused, swallowed. "Charlie was gone. The ghost soldiers took him."

Nobody said anything for a while. Then Art went on, "He must be all right, though. I mean, I've been thinking about it all the way here. Why would they take him away if they were going to . . . I mean, if they meant to hurt him, or worse, they'd have done it there. No, he's a prisoner. A hostage."

Flinch was all for rescuing Charlie there and then. She did not see why they couldn't just go back to Borough station and along the tube lines like before to get him out.

"I imagine he'll be guarded, even assuming that's where he is," Art told her. "No, I'm afraid Charlie will have to wait. I feel bad about it too, but he can look after himself."

"So what do we do?" Meg asked.

"Go to the police?" Jonny suggested.

"No. Well, not yet anyway. Weathers is telling the War Office. I think we'll have to leave it to them. It's their mess, after all."

"But we can't just do nothing," Flinch told them. "We're the Cannoniers. We have to help."

"Tomorrow's Monday," Art said. "That's when Miss Gibson and her people are organizing their exercise against the army. From what Flinch and Charlie have told us—and from what we've seen—it could be a massacre."

"You mean they might ambush Algie's men on the way back from Dartmoor."

"Yes, Jonny, I think it's possible."

"But how will they get to them?" Meg wanted to know. "At the moment all the ghost soldiers are in the secret underground base."

"Unless they've managed to move them out already. So they'll have to evacuate the base tonight."

"Through the haunted house," Jonny suggested.

Art shook his head. "They know that we know about that. And Charlie might have passed on information about it too. No, I think they'll use another route out of their base. One they think we don't know about."

It was dark. Whether by accident or design, the streetlamp outside the entrance to Borough station was not working. The Cannoniers were sitting huddled in a doorway further along the street on the opposite side of the road.

Flinch was shivering with the cold and Meg held her tight. She tried to wrap her own coat around both of them, but it was not really large enough. Soon she was shivering too. It was beginning to seem as if she spent most of her life sitting out in the cold at night.

"Are you sure they'll come this way?" Meg asked.

"No," Art admitted. "But it seems the best bet."

"Maybe one of us should keep watch on the house. In case they use that," Jonny suggested. But he did not sound enthusiastic.

Art was nodding. "Actually," he said. Then he stopped, as if unsure how to continue.

"Actually?" Meg repeated. "Actually what?"

"Actually Flinch is right," Art said after a pause. "We can't just leave Charlie down there with them. And we have to know what's going on." He looked around at them, serious. "I don't know what the War Office will do, if anything. And I don't think we can go to the police—at least, not until we actually see the ghost soldiers coming out of the station and we can show them we aren't just imagining things. The police aren't armed, remember. If they go investigating the house and the secret base, there will be a bloodbath."

Meg could see where this was leading and she was not happy about it. "So you're going back into their base, are you? Through the house. On your own."

Art looked surprised that she had guessed this. "Well, yes."

Meg shook her head. "I know I can't talk you out of it, but I think that's daft."

"Perhaps. But it's what we should do."

"He's right, you know," Jonny put in.

"Are you going with him?" Meg snapped, immediately regretting it as Jonny looked away quickly in embarrassment.

A moment later he turned back to face her, drawn and pale. "If Art wants me to, then yes, I will," he said.

"Thanks." Art put his hand on Jonny's shoulder. "But I need you here. I need you all here." He was looking at Meg, his dark eyes holding hers. "I'll be careful, don't worry. Any trouble and I'll come straight back. But we should do what we can."

"Yes," Flinch agreed enthusiastically. "What do you want us to do, Art?"

"Keep watch here. If I'm not back, and the ghost soldiers or Miss Gibson or anyone you recognize from that secret base comes out, then, Jonny, I want you to follow them. Meg, you go to the nearest police station and get them to send a message to my dad. He's on duty tonight, so they can contact him through Scotland Yard. Get him here—or another policeman. Anyone who can see what's going on and people will listen to." He turned to Flinch. "I want you to help Meg. If there are two of you, they're more likely to listen than if it's just one crazy kid."

"Crazy kid?" Meg muttered. "Thanks!" But she was struggling not to smile. She was always impressed at how

Art could organize them in a few moments and sort out the situation. "You be careful," she told him.

"You too. See you soon." Art grinned as he got to his feet. In a moment he had disappeared into the darkness.

The night grew colder and, if anything, darker. They sat in the doorway, hardly talking. Jonny got bored at one point and ran off down the road, returning a few minutes later from the opposite direction. "Need to keep warm," he told them. "You fancy a run, Flinch?" She didn't.

Neither did Meg. She just wanted to go home and snuggle into bed. But at this time her father would be coming back from the pub, and the thought of meeting him drunk and tired made her shiver again.

"What time do the cleaning people start?" Jonny wondered.

"Art says they're called fluffers," Flinch told him. "He says they have to clean the dust out of the tunnels so there won't be a fire."

"Dust doesn't burn," Meg said.

"It can explode," Jonny said. "If there's a spark from a train and the air's full of dust."

"Hmm," Meg said. She would rather not think about that.

"I don't think anything's going to happen anyway," Jonny said. "The fluffers, or whatever they're called, will be here soon."

As if to confirm his suspicions, the guard they had seen before appeared at the heavy grille across the station entrance. He was whistling cheerfully as he hauled it open. Then he stood for several minutes, still whistling. In between tuneless verses he blew onto his hands and stamped his feet.

"There you are, you see," Jonny said quietly.

"We'll give it another five minutes," Meg said. "Then we'll go and find Art."

She was just about to admit that Art had been wrong and there was no point in staying here in the cold any longer when something did happen. A car drew up outside the station and a man got out. He stood talking to the guard for several minutes. The guard had stopped whistling and his angry voice carried to where Meg, Jonny and Flinch were sitting.

"What am I supposed to tell 'em, eh? I mean, will they get paid or what?"

They continued to talk, more quietly now, and Meg could not hear the guard. He seemed to have been reassured by the other man. Only when the man turned and got back into the car did she see that it was Lawson.

"What was all that about?" Jonny wondered.

"I don't know, but I'm going to find out," Meg decided.

"How?" Flinch wanted to know.

"Easy. I'll ask the guard." The openmouthed looks they gave her were amusing. Before either could recover enough to ask her what she intended to say to him, Meg told them to wait there and then stepped out into the road. She could almost feel Flinch and Jonny's stares as she walked confidently down toward the station.

The guard saw her before she reached him. He watched her approach, frowning. "Oh, it's you again," he said at last. "What do you want?"

"My aunt said to meet her here," Meg told him, making a point of looking around as if she expected her at any moment.

"Yeah, well, you can tell your aunt she can go home again. You too, young lady."

"What?"

"Orders," the guard said importantly. He seemed to gather himself and puff out his chest slightly as he said the word. "There's a repair team coming in later, so they don't want fluffers fluffing about while they're fixing the . . . repairs." He coughed. "Don't worry, she'll be paid same amount as usual on Wednesday."

"Oh." Meg nodded as if this seemed perfectly reasonable. "I'll tell her. Thanks. I suppose," she added as she turned to go, "you'll be supervising the repairs."

The guard laughed. "Not likely. I'm off home too, soon as I've told everyone." He slapped his hands together and stamped his feet again. "Be glad to get in the warm with a nice cup of tea."

The fluffers started to appear a few minutes later. Meg and the others watched them arrive in small groups, talking loudly and laughing to each other. Each group in turn was greeted by the guard. The conversations seemed to follow the same pattern—he would speak to them gravely, puffing his chest out again exactly as he had with Meg. First the fluffers would seem bewildered, then relieved— probably when they were told they would be paid as usual—then they laughed and walked away, chatting as before but now with more animation and amusement.

The guard seemed to know when everyone who was coming had been told about the new arrangements, and he closed the metal grille, locked it and walked away down the road. He had his hands in his pockets and he was whistling again. Somewhere, not quite in time with the tuneless whistling, a clock struck the hour. No wonder it was cold, Meg thought. Three o'clock in the morning on the last day of November.

Within minutes of the guard leaving, the trucks arrived. Their headlights cut through the gloomy night, making it seem somehow cleaner as they washed across the road and over the buildings. One by one they drew up at the curb outside the tube station. Meg was worried they might park along both sides, right next to where she was hiding. She pressed herself back against the cold door, Jonny and Flinch doing the same, as the headlights spilled over the step.

Jonny had been counting. "Five trucks," he said. "Army trucks by the look of it."

Meg thought he was right. They were large, canvas-covered and painted olive green. The air was getting misty from the exhaust fumes as they waited outside the station.

She struggled to see the driver of the truck almost opposite them, but he was a shadowy silhouette. Completely still and silent. Meg had an uncomfortable feeling that if she could see his face it would be the dead, skull-like face of a ghost soldier.

The trucks seemed to wait there forever, engines still running.

"Should we get the police now?" Flinch asked.

"It's just a few trucks," Jonny said. "Let's wait until there's something for them to see."

And so they waited. It seemed like hours before anything else happened. Then a car turned into the street, driving quickly past the trucks and stopping alongside the front one—almost level with the doorway where they were hiding.

It was the same car as before, Meg realized as Lawson got out. She could see him clearly now in the glow of the trucks' headlights. The silver top of his cane glinted and reflected the light as he walked purposefully across the road. He pulled a bunch of keys from his coat pocket and unlocked the grille across the station entrance. With a quick backward glance, as if to reassure himself that the trucks were still there, he stepped through the entranceway and was lost in the shadows.

A few minutes after that the ghost soldiers started to march out.

They could have been an ordinary, well-disciplined army unit. They walked in step, rifles slung over their shoulders, helmets securely on their heads. But as they turned and marched toward the waiting trucks, the light was full on their inhuman faces. The red eyes seemed even deeper set, the jaws even more pronounced, the teeth even sharper. . . . There was a collective hissing from their artificial joints and the air was filled with pale, misty steam. Meg felt Flinch hug her tightly.

"All right," she said. "Time to go. Come on, Flinch. Jonny, if we're not back before they leave, follow them as far as you can."

"We know where they're going," Flinch said.

"We think we do."

"Go on," Jonny urged them. "While they're filling up the back trucks. When they get to this one"—he pointed to the truck almost level with them—"they'll see us."

Meg took Flinch by the hand and they stepped out of the doorway. Flinch gave Jonny a little wave, then they made their way quickly down the road, away from the station and the trucks and the ghost soldiers. They kept close to the buildings, using the shadows, hoping they would not be seen. But it was not until they had turned the corner and were out of sight of the station that Meg even began to relax.

Jonny also stepped out of the doorway, running twenty yards up the road after Meg and Flinch, and ducking into another doorway from where he could watch the trucks without fear of being seen himself. The night was bitterly cold and he was afraid they would see the steam of his breath—he seemed to be making almost as much as the ghost soldiers were.

In less than ten minutes the first of the huge trucks started to rumble forward. Jonny fancied he could see the driver's red eyes glowing through the windshield as it approached and he shrank back into the doorway as the truck passed.

Luckily the trucks did not seem to be moving very fast. They lumbered heavily and noisily along the deserted streets of London. Jonny waited for the last one to pass him, then followed. It was cold, so he was glad of the exercise, jogging easily after the convoy.

He followed it as it gathered speed and confidence through the roads of New Cross and into Lewisham, taking short cuts and using narrow side streets to keep up. The trucks might be doing only about twenty miles an hour, but that was faster than even Jonny could run. He knew that he could not hope to follow them forever, so he tried to picture a map of London in his head. If they really were headed for Dartmoor, which route would they take? Given the fact that they were now almost at Sydenham, he guessed they must be keen to get out of London quickly by going south. Then they would turn west.

One good thing was that in the still of the night he could hear the trucks from a long way off. If he guessed wrong as he tried to leapfrog ahead of them, the sound would fade and he would have to try to get back to it and guess again.

Already the first gentle streaks of dawn were appearing low in the sky. Jonny was losing his breath, having to stop more and more often to take in rasping gulps of cold air. Where were Meg and Flinch? he wondered. Had they managed to persuade the police to come looking for the convoy? And if so, would they find it? Should he look for a telephone box and try to call Art's dad at Scotland Yard to say where he was?

Jonny was working through his options as he skirted Sydenham Park. There was a strange echo to the sound of the convoy now—as if he could hear it coming from two directions. Jonny stopped again, hands on his knees and head down, listening. Something shone in his eyes as he bent and he thought at first it was a truck's headlight. But it was the sun.

The rising sun was behind him, yet the light that had dazzled Jonny for a moment was to the side—glinting, reflecting. He straightened up and shaded his eyes so he could see where it was coming from. It was a building. A huge glass building standing like a giant greenhouse in the park, the sun reflected brilliantly off its side. The Crystal Palace, of course. They had talked about it at school last year—about how the massive glass structure was built for the Great Exhibition over eighty years ago. . . .

But there was no time to remember anything else about

the magnificent building or its history. The sound of the convoy was louder now, and still it seemed to come from both in front of Jonny and behind him.

Ahead of him, the first truck turned onto the road, its headlights dimmed by the gathering light, but still dazzling as they shone full on Jonny. He froze, trapped by the light as another truck turned behind the first. And another. This was crazy. Surely they were heading in the wrong direction—back the way they had come. What was going on? Had they realized they were being followed and come back for him?

Suddenly frightened, Jonny turned to run. But another line of trucks was approaching from the other end of the road. The convoy had split in two to trap him. The only place he could try to hide was against the iron fence at the side of the road and he pressed himself into it. It was too high to climb.

The convoy slowed to a halt about thirty yards away. Jonny waited for the ghost soldiers to come for him, but nothing happened. The trucks just waited. He turned back to the other set of trucks and saw the reason. The door of the leading truck opened and a figure jumped out. The light reflected from the Crystal Palace shone around it like a halo, blurring the detail. But Jonny could see the shape of the soldier's uniform. More of the figures were emerging from the back of the truck and taking up positions beside the first figure.

When he spoke, the figure's voice was clear and loud

and more "human" than Jonny had imagined. "You are ordered to surrender immediately," the voice barked—authoritative and assured. "We have the firepower to enforce that order if necessary."

Jonny swallowed. Slowly, he raised his hands above his head.

Ghost soldiers were disembarking from the rest of the trucks now, the ones at the other end of the road. He could see them clearly—their sunken eyes and pale, bony faces. They arranged themselves into two rows in front of their vehicles. The front row dropped to their knees, rifles unslung and aimed. The second row also aimed their rifles.

"All right—I surrender," Jonny shouted. But his voice was a hoarse whisper, muffled by his terror. He doubted they had heard him.

In unison, the ghost soldiers in the front row worked the bolts on their rifles. Then, as one, they fired.

The study was a "quiet room" where Sarah did her homework or read, and her mother worked when at home. So it seemed the ideal place to escape from Paul's constant stream of nonsensical chatter.

The grown-ups were having coffee and Paul seemed happy to punctuate their conversation with his own. Sarah led Arthur to the study and closed the door behind them.

"He'll come looking for us when he gets bored," she admitted. "Or when Mum gets tired of him and sends him off."

There were two small desks in the room, against opposite walls. Schoolbooks were piled on one of them. A history book was open, facedown, beside a pad of paper with some scrawled notes. The other desk had a computer under it, a flat-screen monitor, keyboard and mouse on the desktop. A shelf on the wall above had computer and software manuals lined up.

"Is that your mum's computer?"

"She uses it as a web server, so it's always on. Broadband, you know."

Arthur nodded. He didn't.

"I use it too. But really it's for her work. So's the study, so I have somewhere else I can go if I have to. She takes a laptop when she's away."

"Is that often?"

Sarah pulled a face, which Arthur supposed meant yes. "She's in Frankfurt next month, and New York in February."

"Do you go with her?"

"She's working. Anyway, I'm at school. And Paul's too young. We go to Dad, usually."

"Is that . . . good?"

She did not answer. Instead she turned over the history book and looked at it for a moment. "This is dire. Doesn't tell you anything, and I have to hand the work in on Tuesday."

Arthur wasn't sure quite what to say. She wasn't really asking for his help, she was avoiding answering his stupid question about her dad. He didn't know what he was doing here. Dad had to leave soon, he was on duty this evening. But it seemed awkward just to stand in silence. So, as a joke really, he said, "Maybe the computer can help."

Sarah lowered the book and looked at him, her lips pursed, her head slightly to one side so that her long black hair hung away from her face and he could just see her ear.

"Why not ask the Invisible Detective?"

She just stared at him.

"You know, like Mr. Hanshaw said at Computer Club."

"Are you trying to be funny?" she snapped. Her eyes were suddenly hard and cold.

"Sorry," Arthur said automatically. Then, "No. I was just trying to help."

Sarah watched him carefully for a while. "Thanks," she said at last. "But I don't think it would help, actually." She seemed to soften again. "So, what do you know about the Invisible Detective?"

Arthur wondered where to start. How could he possibly explain what he knew? He didn't understand it himself. He was saved from having to decide when the door opened.

It was not Paul, though. It was Sarah's mum.

"There you are," she said. "I'm afraid Arthur's dad has to go now. It's been lovely to see you, Arthur. You must come again."

"Yes," Sarah said. "Do." She seemed to mean it. Then, as Arthur was about to follow her mum out, she caught his arm.

"Hang on." She turned on the computer screen. "Let me send you an e-mail."

"OK." He did not object, although it seemed strange to send it while he was there. Maybe she wanted to check his address. She was typing it already.

> Thanks for coming. See you soon.
> S.

"Let me know when it turns up," she said. "You can add me to your address book."

"OK," Arthur said again.

Since Dad was out that afternoon, Arthur checked his e-mail. He was not terribly interested—after all, Sarah's e-mail might not have arrived yet. But it was something to do.

There was one unread e-mail. Arthur stared at it. He felt cold and somehow numb. It couldn't be—could it? He almost didn't open the message. He almost just shut down the machine and went to do something else. Almost.

The e-mail read:

> Thanks for coming. See you soon.
> S.

Just as he knew it would.

But the e-mail address it had come from was not a jumble of letters and numbers like his own. It wasn't even something clever like Sarah@wherever.com, and he realized now why she had thought he was joking. Because Sarah's e-mail address was: BrandonLake@Invisible-Detective.com. Sarah Bustle was the Invisible Detective.

CHAPTER 10

The station sergeant was laughing again. He seemed to have spent most of the time since Meg and Flinch arrived laughing, and it was getting on Meg's nerves.

Flinch seemed unable to comprehend that the policeman just did not believe their story. Everything was so straightforward for her, Meg thought. She had to admit, it was rather an incredible tale. But it annoyed her that he didn't even seem interested. He made no effort to check any of the things she had told him, and he clearly wasn't about to send a policeman with the girls to see these "ghost soldiers" for himself.

"Look, young ladies," he managed between guffaws, "I don't know what you're up to, but you really shouldn't be out at this time in the morning. Why don't you cut along home, eh?"

"Because this is important," Meg told him, through gritted teeth.

The sergeant nodded sympathetically, his mustache twitching as he tried not to break out into another fit of laughter. "Course it is." He leaned across the desk. "Tell you what I'll do. Soon as I go off duty in a couple of hours, I'll nip across to the tube and see these rat men for myself. What do you think about that?" He clearly thought this was a big concession and nodded enthusiastically at his own suggestion.

"I think you'll be too late," Flinch told him seriously. "I think they'll have all gone and people will get hurt. And," she added, "it will be your fault, you silly man."

Meg doubted this was the greatest insult the station sergeant had endured recently, but the seriousness with which Flinch delivered it made him blink with surprise. For a moment, Meg thought it might bring him to his senses enough to listen.

"Look, ladies," he said, his voice hard and all trace of amusement gone, "I've spent a long time listening to your fairy tales, but I have better things to do. So I think you'd best be going before we have to talk about wasting police time and other such matters."

He evidently believed this was the end of the matter. And as if to reinforce the point, the telephone on the desk began to ring.

Meg knew there was no point in staying, but she waited long enough to fix him with her best glare. Except the sergeant was now absorbed in what he was hearing from the telephone. He pulled a pad of paper across the desk and picked up a stub of well-chewed pencil.

"Shooting? Are you sure?"

Meg looked at Flinch and found she was looking back at her. "Has it started?" she whispered. Meg held her hand up as she listened.

"Where?" the sergeant was asking. He caught sight of Meg and Flinch as he spoke, and waved at them impatiently, motioning for them to leave. He turned away, cupping his hand around the phone, as if hoping the view of his back would make the point.

But they had both heard him as he turned, heard where the shooting was. And they both knew that was where they must go: "Sydenham. Crystal Palace Park."

There was a ghost soldier on guard on the porch. Art could see it across the street, a deeper shadow in the darkened doorway. While it was standing there, he could not get into the house. But the fact that the soldier was there at all suggested to him that Miss Gibson and her people still had something to guard, that they had not all evacuated and headed off to Dartmoor.

As well as the laboratory and equipment, Art reckoned that they were guarding Charlie. At least, he hoped they were. He considered returning to Borough station, but dismissed the idea. The others would probably have gone by now in any case. And he would never forgive himself if he missed an opportunity to save Charlie. Having doubted him earlier, Art was all the more convinced now that he must help the man who had helped him so much in the past.

While he waited for an opportunity to slip into the house, Art sat on the low wall opposite, shadowed from the house despite the gray light of dawn. He had considered throwing stones at the sentry, like Flinch had, but he doubted the ghost soldiers would be distracted by the same trick twice and he was on his own now.

He had his casebook in his coat pocket and, while he waited, he wrote up the events so far. He sketched a map of the cellar room, with notes on the opening alcove and secret door. From memory, he drew a floor plan of the rest of the house.

He glanced up from writing, wondering how to describe the operation they had seen performed on the ghost soldier. The light of the rising sun was shining diagonally across the front of the house now, so that it looked less forbidding, less like a skull. It was only as he started writing again that Art realized what he had not seen.

The sentry was gone.

He looked back quickly, stuffing the casebook and his pencil into his coat pocket. There was no doubt about it—the porch was deserted. With a glance up and down the street, Art jumped off the wall and hurried across to the house. He hesitated outside the gate before running to the porch.

Once there, he held his breath and listened. There was no sound. Carefully, he tried the door—ready to turn and run as soon as he heard or saw anything threatening inside. Of course, the door would be locked anyway. But it was worth a try before he turned his attention to the window and tried to force his way through the narrow gap there.

The door opened easily and quietly. Nervously, Art pushed it open and looked inside. The hallway was empty. It was silent inside, not even the rumble of a distant tube train. Could it really be this easy? He stepped inside the house, looking up the stairs, searching for telltale shadows or the sound of movement. But there was nothing.

Nothing, until the front door slammed shut behind him. Art spun around—to find the sentry standing by the door. It had its rifle leveled and its deep, red eyes glared at Art, as if daring him to move.

It had taken Jonny a full minute, cowering against the fence with his hands over his head, to realize they were not firing at him.

The ghost soldiers were firing at the other soldiers. It was only when he saw one of the troops from the further convoy throw his hands up and collapse in a heap that Jonny realized what was happening. Only then did he see that the soldiers from the other convoy were human. He didn't know what was going on, who these soldiers were or what they were trying to do. But at least now he knew which way to run.

Jonny kept close to the fence. Bullets whistled past him, one chipping the pavement at his feet and sending fragments of concrete stinging up at him. The troops he was running toward seemed to be outnumbered. They had retreated behind their trucks. As Jonny raced for cover, the front truck lurched suddenly sideways, as if trying to dodge a bullet. Jonny heard the crack as its front driver's-side tire exploded.

One of the soldiers was shouting at the others. But his words were lost in the storm of gunfire. As Jonny ran toward them, the troops seemed to retreat almost as fast. The ghost soldiers were advancing down the street, not seeming to care that they were leaving dead and dying comrades behind them. In a sudden flash of insight, Jonny realized that this was what made them so effective—and so inhuman. . . .

The commander of the soldiers opposing them was waving to his men to get off the road and away from the vehicles. Jonny did not understand why until one of them exploded. Ammunition, he thought, as the whole truck was consumed in an orange fireball. The cab seemed to lift off the wheels to allow a mass of flame to emerge from underneath it. In an instant the canvas covering was gone, leaving only a blackened skeleton of metal supports. The truck continued to burn, black smoke drifting across the road and covering the soldiers' retreat.

Jonny almost ran past them. Then he caught a fleeting glimpse of a dark figure crossing his path and saw that they were actually making their way into Crystal Palace Park.

"Regroup by the main entrance to the palace," he heard a voice crying out. "We have to draw them in and then keep them bottled up until reinforcements arrive."

The voice sounded confident. But somewhere close by, smothered by the drifting smoke, Jonny heard a mutter of, "What reinforcements?"

There was a cloying, choking smell of cordite from the burning munitions. Somewhere in the muffled distance behind him, Jonny heard another explosion and the smoke thickened. The fire was spreading to the other trucks.

He was standing beside one of the heavy metal gates into the park. Figures loomed out of the fog of dark smoke. Seeing the helmet, the leveled rifle, the backpack, Jonny almost ran over to join them. But then he caught sight of the burning coals that were the nearest figure's eyes and instead he ducked behind the gatepost. He ran, not knowing where he was or where he was going. It seemed to be downhill, but that might just be his fear and panic propelling him forward.

Another shape now—dark in the thinning smoke. Jonny skidded to a halt as a head emerged. A huge, monstrous face with jutting jaw and horn. Glassy eyes stared at him hungrily. A dinosaur, one enormous claw raised and ready to slash at him. They faced each other, both motionless in disbelief. Like statues.

Then Jonny realized that it was a statue. Crystal Palace Park—fountains and life-sized statues of animals, dinosaurs even. He almost laughed. Almost, because at that moment the renewed sound of gunfire tore through the smoky air and jolted him back to reality. Jonny grinned foolishly at the dinosaur statue and gave it a half wave.

The smoke seemed to be clearing, although perhaps it was just that his eyes were adjusting to the misty world of the park. Blurred in the distance, Jonny could see a figure in uniform. It was moving away from him, so he could not see the face—could not tell if it was human or . . .

Another figure appeared behind the first, silhouetted for a moment against the gray mist, teeth clearly visible and sunken eyes glowing greedily. It raised its rifle.

"Look out!" The shout surprised Jonny. He had not even realized he was going to call out.

The ghost soldier hesitated, turning toward the sound—toward Jonny. The figure in front of it was turning too, a mirror action. A revolver was swinging up, just as the ghost soldier's rifle was seeking out Jonny.

Jonny dived to the ground as a shot rang out. But it was not the ghost soldier's rifle. It was the revolver. At the same moment, it seemed, the ghost soldier lurched forward, as if throwing itself at Jonny. It staggered forward, then crashed to the ground, its inhuman face close to Jonny's on the glistening grass.

A hand grabbed Jonny by the shoulder and hauled him to his feet. "Who the devil are you? What are you doing here?" It was the same voice that had been shouting orders.

"I was following the ghost soldiers," Jonny stammered.

"Ghost soldiers?" The soldier nudged the dead creature with the toe of his boot. "Good description. What are these things?"

"Some sort of experiment," Jonny explained. The sound of the battle seemed to have receded into the distance as they spoke. The smoke was clearing and he could see the face of the young soldier beneath his helmet where previously there had been only shadow. It was a grim, determined face. It reminded him of someone. . . . "That's what Charlie said, anyway."

"Charlie?" The soldier seemed surprised.

"Lord Fotherington."

"Charlie," the soldier repeated. "Uncle Charlie." He was shaking Jonny's hand. "Are you Art?"

"Jonny. A friend of Art's."

"Captain Algernon Maltravers," the soldier told him. "Algie. Let's get to the palace and find the others. Now tell me, what exactly is going on?"

There were perhaps a dozen soldiers outside the huge glass doors. Jonny had never been to the Crystal Palace, though his father had once talked about taking them. He was astonished at how big it was, towering above him and stretching far into the distance. So much glass. Even obscured by the drifting smoke, it glinted and shone in the stray shafts of sunlight that filtered through.

One of the solders ran up to Algie and saluted. "Most of the lads are taking cover and trying to hold them back, sir. We're regrouping on the road behind the Crystal Palace."

"Good," Algie told him. "I want you to hold them here as long as you can, Sergeant."

"Where are you going, sir?" He seemed to catch sight of Jonny for the first time. "And who's this?"

"This is Jonny—he knows something of what's going on. I'm going for help, Sergeant. At least, I'm going to rescue the one man who can organize the help we really need."

Algie took two other soldiers with him, leaving instructions for Sergeant Barker to engage the enemy and prevent them from leaving the park. Jonny quickly told Barker everything he had already told Algie.

"And they said we were going on maneuvers against another crack unit," the sergeant said. "They weren't kidding."

The sound of gunfire was getting closer as the day progressed. Jonny had not realized that being scared could be so boring. For hours they sat listening to the guns and the incoming reports as soldiers ran over with updates on the fighting. By late morning, the sun was breaking through the smoke as it dispersed and Jonny could see a line of ghost soldiers working its way across the park, up toward the huge glass building where they were sheltering.

"It's no use," Barker decided at last. "We need more cover."

"In there?" Jonny asked.

"There's nowhere else. They've got us cut off from the main group now. Johnson, get those doors open. We'll draw them inside and try to keep them busy till the captain gets back." He turned back to Jonny. "It's obvious we're outnumbered, but do you know how many of them there are?"

Jonny tried to think. He had counted the trucks outside the tube station. How many ghost soldiers had got into each truck? "I don't know," he admitted. "Maybe fifty?"

"Fifty?" Barker shook his head. "Is that all," he muttered. Then he winked at Jonny. "Actually, that's not so bad." He paused as a bullet crashed through a panel of glass behind them, shattering it into a thousand pieces. "They're getting a bit close for comfort. Are those doors open yet?" he yelled.

Barker waited to make sure the few soldiers in his team were inside before he followed. Jonny waited with him, despite the burly sergeant trying to shoo him inside. "It's not so bad, son," Barker said. "They don't seem to have much initiative and they're not worried about avoiding casualties. Seems some guy with a top hat and cane is directing operations from the rear."

"Lawson."

"If you say so. Now come on—it won't take them long to realize we're inside and they're shooting at nothing. With luck, most of the lads will have regrouped on the road and be waiting for orders. Let's hope these ghost soldiers concentrate on the main group and not us. The rest of the lads'll finish them off easy."

There was a circular raised pond in the entrance hall and Jonny caught a glimpse of goldfish swimming lazily around in the clear water. As if they too were under glass. Then Barker grabbed his collar and dragged him away.

The firing continued outside, more and more panes of

glass disintegrating under the approaching assault. Despite the fact that the whole building was made of glass, it seemed strangely dark inside. It was a blur to Jonny as he followed the soldiers into the depths of the building.

Barker pointed out areas of cover for his men, the idea being, so far as Jonny could tell, that they would retreat slowly through the main concourse of the building, picking off as many ghost soldiers as they could—until either there were none left or reinforcements from the main group arrived.

As Barker and Jonny took cover behind a statue of Queen Victoria, the world seemed suddenly calm and quiet. Beside him, Barker caught his breath and Jonny realized that the sound of shooting had stopped.

"It didn't take them long to work out we'd gone," Barker said quietly. "Now, will they leave us alone or try to finish us off as we're trapped?"

Almost as soon as he finished speaking, the main doors at the end of the long, wide concourse exploded in a hailstorm of icy fragments. Jonny ducked away as the sharp points of glass lashed through the air around them. When he dared to look back, he saw smoke billowing through the shattered doors. And through the smoke came the ghost soldiers.

They were in the room where Art had seen the first ghost soldier being operated on. It seemed so long ago, so much had happened since then. He and Charlie were sitting on a bench at the side of the room, with one of the ghost soldiers standing guard over them.

In the middle of the room, Miss Gibson was talking quietly to two scientists in white coats. There was a radio-telephone on a table in the corner of the room and another scientist was getting updates on the battle at Sydenham and relaying the relevant information to Miss Gibson. She seemed pleased with the way things were going.

One day, Art thought as he watched, you won't need a huge box with a telephone receiver on the side and a big antenna out of the top like that to communicate without wires. Just a handset with everything built in. He wasn't sure how he knew this, but he was as certain of it as he was of anything.

"If only we could get out of here," Charlie said quietly, "I could get the War Office to send reinforcements to help Algie and his men." From the news over the radio-telephone, it seemed that the troops had taken refuge inside the Crystal Palace itself. Miss Gibson had told Lawson, who was in charge of matters at Sydenham, to get the local police to cordon off the area. It was Sunday, so the Crystal Palace would be closed anyway.

Art watched as the man at the radio-telephone scribbled another note for Miss Gibson. "Could we signal for help with that?" he asked Charlie.

"Possibly. If either of us knew how to work it."

That was a point. If they just shouted into it, only Lawson would hear. They would have had to retune it somehow to some army or government frequency. Jonny would have been able to do it—he had made a crystal set at home, he'd told Art proudly once—but Art had no idea about such things.

"What's going to happen to us?" he asked Charlie.

But it was Miss Gibson who answered. Art had not noticed her approach. "You're going to die," she said simply. "Once all this is over and I'm sure I have no further use for you."

"You're mad," Charlie told her. "You really think killing us—and all those soldiers—will somehow help you?"

"Oh, I'm sure it will. A successful exercise on this scale will guarantee—"

Charlie cut her off. "Guarantee you get locked away and this hideous experiment is closed down."

Her nostrils flared and her eyes widened. She took a step forward and slapped Charlie across the face with her hand. He gasped in surprise, putting his own hand to his cheek.

"Or I may not wait. I may just kill you both now." She stared at them. "Yes, perhaps that would be best. There would be some satisfaction in letting you wait until my victory is complete, but it isn't strictly necessary." From her jacket pocket she produced a pistol and aimed it at Charlie. The muzzle was barely a foot from his face.

"Kill me if you like," he said quietly. "But that won't alter the facts. You're still mad."

Her eyes widened again and the color drained from

her face. Art could see her knuckles whiten as she began to squeeze the trigger. In that moment, he knew she was about to fire—about to kill Charlie. He closed his eyes tight and the sound of the shot echoed around the room.

The palace was a mixture of exhibitions and storerooms, so far as Jonny could tell. It was also filling with smoke, so that the early-afternoon sun was misty and pale through the high, vaulted ceilings. With the smoke and the sun and the lack of ventilation, it was getting hot and stuffy.

Barker's men retreated slowly through the huge building, picking off ghost soldiers as they went. But still there seemed to be more and more of them. Several of Barker's soldiers had been shot down. One of the survivors was carrying a radio-telephone on his back, but a shot from a ghost soldier had torn a hole in the heavy pack, exposing the innards.

"We're going to be trapped in the south tower if we're not careful," a soldier told Barker as they fell back another ten yards.

There was a large exhibition hall off to the side of the concourse. At first Jonny thought it was full of people, but they were standing completely still. Waxworks, he realized. The entrance was guarded by two figures—one was a soccer player in shorts and purple shirt, his right foot resting on a heavy leather ball. The other was a cricketer in full whites, holding his bat as if ready to walk to the crease.

"Can't we just smash our way out?" Jonny suggested.

"In here maybe?" But he was not even sure they had heard him. Barker led them past the waxworks hall without sparing it a look.

A group of ghost soldiers hurled themselves forward into a flurry of bullets. Three of them fell, but others were still coming, firing from the hip as they ran. Their movement was strangely graceful, like sleek animals rather than battle-weary troops.

Barker waved for his men to fall back again. "See if we can make a stand at the intersection." A corridor joined the main concourse here, perhaps the route to the south tower the soldier had mentioned.

Jonny belted along the concourse and hurled himself around the corner. But the corridor was not empty. Two figures were emerging, walking toward him, and Jonny stopped, staring in disbelief.

Moments later, Sergeant Barker and two other soldiers joined him, and they too stood openmouthed as they caught sight of the figures.

"Hello, Jonny," said Meg. "Having fun? You're making enough noise."

"We came as quick as we could," Flinch said. "Honest. But we didn't know where you were till we saw the ghost soldiers."

The shot seemed strangely distant. There were shouts, more shots, and Art opened his eyes.

Charlie was still sitting beside him, unharmed. The ghost soldier that had been standing guard over them was a crumpled heap on the floor. Miss Gibson had swung around in surprise. Art turned to see where she and Charlie were looking. On the opposite side of the room, a uniformed soldier was sighting along his revolver. In the open area outside the room, Art could see another two soldiers in similar positions, with rifles leveled, keeping watch on the corridors.

Almost immediately, one of the soldiers reeled and fell as another shot rang out.

"Algie?" Charlie gasped.

"Come on!" the soldier shouted.

But Charlie seemed unable to move. Art was already on his feet. He grabbed hold of Charlie's hand and pulled him up. Then he ran, as fast as he could, at Miss Gibson. She was bringing her pistol up again and Art cannoned into her as she fired.

Two shots—one from Miss Gibson's pistol, another from the soldier, from Algie. Miss Gibson's shot went wide, smashing into the wall of the room. The second shot punched through the air where she had been, close to Art's ear. Too close—he felt the breeze as it passed.

Then he and Charlie were running. The white-coated scientists were diving for cover. Algie was firing again, and a chair spun across the room as a shot caught it. A glass jar exploded, viscous green liquid spilling onto the floor.

They were out of the room now. Charlie was ahead of Art and Algie was behind them, still firing. But Miss Gibson was sheltering behind an overturned table.

A soldier lay prone on the floor, his eyes staring and empty. Another grabbed Charlie and propelled him toward the station area. Art made to follow, but a ghost soldier emerged at that moment from the corridor, blocking the way. Art dived to one side as the creature snarled with rage and fired without aiming.

One of the scientists was running from the room and the ghost soldier's shot caught him in the chest. The impact lifted the man and hurled him back into the room—just as Algie was running for the door. The scientist's body hit Algie and knocked him sideways.

"Run!" he shouted as he fell.

The ghost soldier snarled again and fired another shot. The soldier who had pushed Charlie out and was now racing for the platform seemed to freeze at the sound. Then his back arced inward, his head snapped back in surprise and he crashed to the ground, close to his dead comrade.

Art did not wait, he ran.

But another ghost soldier was already on the platform. Art could see Charlie waiting by the stairs at the far end—could see the ghost soldier aiming at him.

"Sydenham!" Art yelled. "Get to Sydenham! I'll see you there."

Charlie disappeared up the stairs and a moment later

the brickwork behind where he had been standing exploded into fragments.

The ghost soldier turned back toward Art. But there was no one there.

Crouched below the platform, keeping clear of the rails, Art held his breath and listened. Had Charlie got away? Were there more ghost soldiers on guard in the house above, waiting for him?

Whether there were or not, Art was trapped in the base now. Alone. He could hear Algie shouting, though the words were indistinct. Then there was another shot, and a thud, and silence.

There was nothing on TV and Arthur was bored. He thought of sending Sarah Bustle an e-mail, but he didn't know what to put in it.

Eventually, he picked up the Invisible Detective's case-book. The cover was scratched and worn, pitted with age. The pages were yellowing and brittle under his fingers. He lay on his bed and leafed through the notebook, glancing at the scrawled pencil and ink, and the hand-drawn diagrams and sketches. But he wasn't really taking anything in.

Somewhere in a drawer in the bedside cabinet was a stone, a round flat disk of some mineral that reflected myriad colors and seemed to deepen when you held it to the light. He was tempted to get it out and stare into the shifting patterns. But he knew he would lose himself in it. He would feel himself drifting back and dreaming of . . . who knew what? Better to read the book.

Odd words and phrases stood out and he worked his way through the pages, his mind drifting—thinking about Sarah and the e-mail. . . . "Jonny . . . Flinch . . . Meg . . . Cannoniers . . ." Another page, another drawing—the front of a shop this time. *Edax Rerum* it said above the door in block pencil letters shaded in gray.

"Clock." He had turned the page before he realized what he had seen and read. The clock. He had left it in the house—the haunted house—when he ran away. Arthur shrank back into the bed as he remembered, suddenly embarrassed that he had got so spooked. Even though there was no one there, he glanced around and felt like hiding under the covers.

The clock. It was still at the house. He did not know how or if it was important, but it had Meg's name scratched off the back. There was something familiar about the clock. Something he had read. One of the cases that he was somehow not yet ready to remember perhaps?

Arthur turned back through the book. But it was no good. He could not settle to reading. The text was too small and too difficult to decipher, even though the handwriting was identical to his own. Suddenly the room seemed stuffy—he needed to get out, get some air. Go for a walk, just wander. And he knew already where he would end up.

The clock was where he had dropped it, in the hall close to the door down to the cellar. The flashlight beam found it at once, and Arthur picked it up and examined it. The hands were still. It was not ticking. For a moment he considered winding it up again, but he decided not to. It was a struggle to work the clock into his coat pocket, but eventually he got it past the tight opening and it dropped inside, pulling his collar heavily to one side.

There was just one more thing that Arthur wanted to do. Well, "wanted" was not really the word, he thought as he slowly climbed the stairs. But he had to check. The door would be locked, of course. Just check, quickly, then go home.

The landing corridor seemed longer than before. The door to the end room was closed, but seemed further away than he remembered. The light of the flashlight was pale and faint by the time it reached the door. And as he approached, it seemed as if he were getting no closer. Until, suddenly, he was there—standing in front of the door, his hand on the doorknob.

Arthur turned the knob and pushed. The door swung slowly open. He was tempted to turn and run—again. But he forced himself to step inside the room and shine the flashlight around. Just a room, an empty room, like all the others, with broken furniture and faded, threadbare curtains.

Except it wasn't like that.

The room was clean. The bare boards showed no trace of dust. There was a desk against one wall, with a modern office chair beside it. Books and papers were piled on one side. Before he knew it, Arthur was standing beside the desk, shining the flashlight down at the pile of books. On the top was a textbook. It looked just like the book he used for history—same shape, size, color. . . . He picked it up, though his fingers were as numb as his mind and he almost dropped it. Just like his history book, it had his school's name printed across the front in block capitals.

"I thought you'd be back."

Arthur did drop the book now. He swung around in a panic, feeling his heart beating in his chest, a sudden cold in his bones. The flashlight wavered, danced and eventually found the doorway. Found the figure standing there.

She was leaning against the door frame, her arms folded. Her face was set in a stern, almost sulky expression and her head was tilted slightly to one side, so that her long, straight hair fell away.

For a second she reminded Arthur of someone else, though he could not think who—her mother perhaps. Then Sarah pushed herself away from the door frame with a flick of the shoulder and stepped into the room.

"Come to help with my homework?" she suggested. "Or to ask about the Invisible Detective?"

CHAPTER 11

Art had no idea how long he had been crouched below the platform. He might have stayed there all day, except that after a while he heard a faint humming sound from the rails behind him. It was a high-pitched whine at first, barely audible. He was still trying to work out what it was when the tone changed, deepened and merged with a distant rumble.

With sudden realization, Art stood up, checking the area was clear, then clambered quickly onto the platform. The sound was much closer now—building to a roar. Seconds later, the dark circle of the tunnel was illuminated by the lights of the approaching train. He caught flashing glimpses of the people in the carriages—reading the paper, sitting with bored expressions, occasionally chatting, but all oblivious to his presence.

If the train had slowed, he might have been tempted to try to leap on the back and escape through the tunnels. But it did not and in a moment it was gone.

Art's first inclination was to make for the stairs and get into the house. But as the train rumbled into the distance, he realized that he could still hear a low humming sound. Cautiously, he made his way along to the archway that led through to the main area of the base. The sound grew louder as he approached.

It was coming from the laboratory. The open area outside the room was empty, but Art could see there were several people inside the lab. Miss Gibson was talking loudly, above the sound of the equipment. Several of the white-coated scientists were grouped around the large table in the middle of the room. There was a line of ghost soldiers at the back of the room. They were standing to attention, for all the world as if they were on a parade ground.

He did not know how many people—and ghost soldiers—were left in the base, but whatever they were doing would have to wait, Art decided. He was getting out while they were occupied.

Even as he reached this conclusion, even as he started to turn away, one of the scientists moved and Art was able to see past him into the room—able to see the table where he had watched the ghost soldier being created. . . . And he could see that again there was a figure lying on the table, arms and legs strapped down and head slightly raised. It was Algie.

There were, Jonny realized with a shock, just three soldiers left—Sergeant Barker and two privates. One was called Jimmy, the other Ted. It was Ted who had the heavy radio-telephone, but despite his efforts to call for reinforcements, the device seemed to be damaged beyond repair. The ghost soldiers were advancing more cautiously now, having also suffered heavy casualties.

Barker seemed at a loss as to what to do now that they

had been joined by two girls. Jonny guessed he was torn between trying to protect them and mounting a final glorious attack on the ghost soldiers who had killed almost all his men.

"Why don't we hide," Flinch suggested, "and wait till they go away?"

"Or at least keep out of their way until help arrives?" Jonny added.

"If it arrives," Ted muttered. He had given up on the radio-telephone now, though he seemed loath to leave it behind.

Barker glared at him. "That's enough of that."

"There's rooms full of junk back there where we got in," Flinch said.

"Got in?" Barker considered this. "Maybe we can get out without them knowing, leave them wandering around inside looking for us." He was already leading them back the way that Flinch and Meg had come, toward the south tower.

"It was a window," Meg said. "Flinch got through easily, but I only just managed."

"Doesn't matter," Jimmy told her. "The walls are glass. We can shoot a hole in them if we need to."

"Then why don't you?"

Jimmy and Ted exchanged looks, but neither of them spoke. It was Barker who answered Meg's question. "Because, miss, our orders are to keep those things busy and bottled up. Once they finish with us, or if they think we've gone, there's no knowing who they'll turn on next or what damage they'll do."

Ted shrugged. "And orders is orders," he said, as if that settled the matter so far as he was concerned.

There was a door across the entrance to the south tower. It had a sign on it: Baird Television Company. Positively No Admittance.

"Television," Jimmy pronounced carefully. "What's that all about, then?"

"I told you—it's a load of junk, that's all," Flinch said as she heaved the door open.

Barker closed the door behind them, bolting it. "Not that it'll make much odds," he observed.

Almost as soon as he finished speaking, several shots slammed into the other side of the door and the wood cracked. A splinter flew out, whipping past Jonny's cheek. "Now what?"

"Now we get you kids out of here," Barker said. "Me and the lads'll stay till you or the captain gets back with help."

The door was shaking under the impact of bullets now, the wood shredding away. Barker led them at a run along the corridor. The rooms full of junk that Flinch had mentioned were laboratories, workshops and studios, Jonny saw, as they raced past. Electrical equipment, glass screens, huge cameras . . . The outside walls were still made of glass, but the inside rooms had been built out of wooden and plaster screens. Some of them had low, false ceilings, while others seemed to stretch up forever toward the cloudy sky. Already it was getting dark.

"Just through here," Meg said as they reached an intersection.

But Barker grabbed her and pulled her back. A split second later, a bullet shattered a glass wall behind where Meg had been standing, the whole massive sheet of glass collapsing in on itself like a waterfall of ice. The sound it made reminded Jonny of a rain stick he had made once out of a cardboard tube filled with gravel.

A group of ghost soldiers had appeared from the end of the corridor and were marching toward them.

"Where did they come from?" Jimmy demanded.

The air was thick with gunfire now. Ted loosed off a round, then ducked back around the corner.

"In here, quick!" Barker shoved Meg and Flinch into a room and Jonny followed a moment later. "They must have gone around the outside and smashed their way in to get ahead of us."

The room was not big and the space was all but filled with a workbench covered in a mass of electrical equipment. Wires and valves were piled on almost every inch of the surface, and the floor was littered with cardboard boxes full of more equipment. The walls seemed pretty solid, stretching up for about fifteen feet, and the door was made of heavy wood. There was a floor above them, probably many floors in the high tower, but the ceiling was well above the top of the walls. Once the whole area had been open, probably exhibition space like the rest of the palace.

Jimmy backed into the room after Barker, firing as he came. Ted was close behind him, hefting the radio-telephone on his shoulders. The sound of shooting was almost deafening. As soon as he was inside, Barker slammed the heavy door shut and bolted it. The sounds from outside were only slightly diminished.

"Dr. Lawson reports that they are down to just a dozen. But they have the remains of the army unit trapped."

Miss Gibson received this news without any apparent change of expression so far as Art could see as he watched from outside the room.

"They should have finished the soldiers off by now," she called across to the man sitting beside the radio-telephone. "Tell him to finish the job, then get back here." She was standing beside the table, looking down at Algie.

He was conscious, staring up at her with undisguised contempt. "You won't find Sergeant Barker so easy to finish off."

"No?" Miss Gibson seemed amused. "I would say that so far my enhanced troops have been more than a match for your so-called crack unit."

"And how many of them has it taken? How many have you lost? What sort of casualty rate do you think is acceptable?"

Art saw her expression change now. Miss Gibson

snarled with rage, her face contorted for a moment so she was almost like one of the ghost soldiers. Then she slapped Algie across the face. "The exercise has been a tremendous success," she hissed. "My troops will be the finest in the British Army."

"If there are any left. Down to a dozen, wasn't it?"

Miss Gibson stared down at him for a long moment. Then she turned to one of the scientists. "Is the new conversion drug ready yet?"

The scientist nodded. "We estimate the new formula will speed up the process considerably. Of course, we haven't tested it yet."

"Then we shall test it now," Miss Gibson told him.

"Now? But we haven't completed the trials."

"Now," she insisted. "While we have such an unwilling test subject."

Art did not like the sound of this. He did not want to see what was going to happen, but at the same time he could not bring himself to leave Algie. He struggled to think how he could help, but with the ghost soldiers and the scientists in the room he was powerless, and there was no time to get help—even if he knew who to turn to. In any case, Charlie would be doing all he could.

One of the scientists had a syringe. He held it up to the light and pushed the plunger slightly until a thin jet of clear liquid squirted from the top. As he turned toward Algie, Miss Gibson took the syringe from him.

"What are you doing?" Algie sounded worried now,

shrinking away from the woman, trying to pull his arm out of her reach but held by the straps across the table.

She stuck the syringe into his upper arm, through his shirt. "We need to know if our new formula is effective." She removed the needle and Algie seemed to slump back on the table. "And since you are so concerned for the safety of my soldiers, I think that perhaps you should lead them in the final assault."

Art strained to see Algie's face. He could not make out his expression—it seemed he was frowning, shaking his head as he strained at the straps that held him down.

"Never," he gasped. But it was an obvious effort to speak. His voice was rough and broken. "What have you done to me?" His eyes seemed to have turned red with the effort. "You animal!"

Miss Gibson was laughing, although none of the scientists joined in. "One of us is an animal. But it isn't me." She turned to a scientist. "Are you ready to operate as soon as the transformation is stabilized?"

He nodded, saying nothing. Another scientist brought a low trolley over from the other side of the table and Art could see it had one of the battery backpacks on it. There was also a pile of metal rods, leg braces and other things he could not see—and did not want to.

Art's attention was on Algie. He was not frowning, but somehow his eyebrows were lower and his red eyes had receded into his face, so that it seemed taut, cadaverous, like a skull. He was opening and closing his mouth, but no words came. Instead there was a growling, moaning sound. His teeth seemed to be growing out over the gums and dark stubble was bristling on his chin and cheeks.

With a sudden howl of rage, Algie sat up. The straps across the table snapped in succession like a burst of machine-gun fire. Algie stared across the room, and although he was looking straight at Art, his deep red eyes were unfocused. Dead. It seemed as if, now that he was free, Algie had no idea what to do next. He just sat there, with his dead eyes. His face was an expressionless mask. The face of a ghost soldier.

Art turned and ran.

The shooting had stopped and now there was a steady "thump" from the other side of the door. Barker and Jimmy had pushed the heavy workbench up against it, but even this was shuddering under the impact. Were they using a battering ram? Meg wondered.

Jonny seemed almost in a world of his own. He had found a way to turn on several large lamps that looked like spotlights. They were mounted on what seemed to be the sort of tripods photographers used, and they cast long shadows across the floor and walls. Now, together with Ted, he was going through the various cardboard boxes and dragging out strange-looking electrical components as if it were Christmas already. She felt like telling them there was almost another month yet.

But Meg was more worried about Flinch. She was walking slowly around the small room, looking up at the high partition walls, also in a world of her own. Meg walked beside the younger girl for a complete circuit of the room before she asked quietly, "Flinch, are you all right?"

"We have to get out," Flinch said, still staring up toward the high ceiling.

"We will. Help will be here soon."

"I can get help." Flinch looked at Meg. She was grinning. "That wall's easiest. Look." She pointed at the back wall of the room. "It's furthest from where the ghost soldiers are and there's a couple of handholds near the top."

Meg could just see the shadowy breaks in the smooth surface, where the wooden panel was damaged. "What are you thinking?"

"Easy. I climb out over the wall, and go and get help."

Jimmy and Sergeant Barker were standing beside them now. "That sounds dangerous," Jimmy said.

"Safer than staying in here," Barker pointed out. "Can you climb that high?"

"If you lift me as far as you can, I can get a hold and do the rest."

"And how will you get out of the building?"

Flinch shrugged. "Same way me and Meg got in."

"If Flinch says she can do it, she can," Jonny called across.

He had built a pile of bits and pieces from the boxes on the edge of the workbench. Ted had removed the radio-telephone from his back and set it down next to Jonny's hoard. The pile wobbled as the bench shifted again. The bolt was working loose from the top of the door and soon the ghost soldiers outside would have to move only the weight of the bench.

There was a brief debate about whether Sergeant Barker could actually lift Jimmy or Ted high enough to get over the wall and go with Flinch. But Meg pointed out that they would then be on their own when Flinch escaped through the window, or risk being heard if they tried to smash their way out with her. Better, she suggested, that Flinch sneak out on her own—so long as Flinch was happy to go.

Flinch was hopping from one foot to the other, eager to get started. Barker lifted her onto his shoulders and held her ankles tight as Flinch stood up. She was still not quite tall enough to reach the top of the wall, but she somehow braced her fingers into the small dents high up the wall and hauled herself up and off Barker's shoulders. The sergeant stood underneath her, arms raised ready to catch her if she fell.

But it was obvious that Flinch was not going to fall. She scrambled up the wall as if she were actually crawling along the floor. Meg could not imagine how she managed to keep her hold, but soon she was hooking her arm over the top and pulling herself up with a grin of triumph.

Flinch looked down the other side of the wall. Meg

could see her face clearly—could see her grin of delight freeze, then fade. Flinch screamed, let go of the wall and fell.

Barker caught her and they both tumbled to the floor. But Meg hardly noticed. Where Flinch had been just seconds ago there was now another figure. The skull face of a ghost soldier rose above the wall and stared down at them. Its clawlike gloved hands reached down toward them, and Meg realized the creature was about to launch itself off the top and leap down at them.

A shot. For the briefest instant, the terrible thing was still there, looking down at them. Then it seemed to shatter, the red eyes spreading out. Its hands left the wall and clamped over its face, frozen for a moment before it disappeared with a shriek of pain. There was a crash from the other side of the wall, a roar of sound like someone falling down stairs. It seemed to go on forever. Jimmy lowered his rifle.

"Well done, lad," Barker said to Jimmy, clapping him on the shoulder. "You'd best keep an eye on the walls. In case they try again." He turned to Flinch. "You all right, miss?"

She nodded. "They had tables and chairs piled up." Her face was white. "There were lots of them, climbing up the other side."

"Looks like we're stuck here, then," Meg said.

She had been sure that Flinch would get help, but now she felt numb and dazed. Ted was looking down at Jonny, who was sitting cross-legged on the floor, playing with some of the bits and pieces he had found in the boxes. She was suddenly angry that he could be so calm. Usually he was the nervous one, first to panic. Perhaps he was coping by ignoring the danger they were in—simply blotting it from his mind.

"What are you doing?" she demanded.

Jonny looked up, apparently surprised that everyone was now staring at him. "Who, me?"

"Yes," Meg snapped. "You."

He told her. She stood for a moment, mouth hanging open in astonishment. She was half aware that Jimmy, Barker and Flinch were wearing similar expressions. "You have to be joking," she said.

Charlie was angry. Art could see that at once. The station sergeant was also angry, and it looked as if the two of them had been shouting at each other for a while before Art arrived at the police station.

"You can call who you like, sir," the policeman was saying, "but I have instructions from the highest level. Dr. Lawson from the Ministry has officially asked that the area be cordoned off for important maneuvers. Secret maneuvers."

"Dr. Lawson is not from the Ministry," Charlie insisted. "He has no official status at all."

"That's not my information, sir."

"You mean, that isn't what he told you."

"Sir," the red-faced policeman said, "I have no proof

that you have any official position. Just the ramblings of a couple of girls and your own rather strange assertions."

"Girls?" Art said, relieved that at least something was going well. "You mean, Meg and Flinch are here?"

But Charlie's grave expression dispelled his optimism. "They were here. This . . ." He seemed to be struggling to find a suitable word to describe the station sergeant. "This buffoon here sent them away."

"What? Where did they go? And where's Jonny?"

"Look," the policeman insisted, "I cannot act against someone who seems to have all the proper credentials just on the say-so of you two and your friends. You may be right. There was something fishy about that Lawson man— altogether too smug, if you ask me. But I need proof that there really is an emergency before I contact this Drake chap at the Yard, or War Office, or anyone."

He seemed pleased at this sensible-sounding proposition, obviously hoping it would calm Charlie and Art down.

Charlie, looking anything but calm, took a deep breath. "And what, apart from a gun battle raging in Crystal Palace Park and the word of a peer of the realm, would it take to convince you?"

The station sergeant frowned at this, but he was saved from answering as another policeman came into the room.

"Sarge, we've got something funny here," the policeman said. He caught sight of Charlie and grinned sheepishly. "You still here, sir?"

Charlie scowled.

"You going to share the joke, Meadows?" the sergeant asked. "We're rather busy here, as you can see."

"Yes, sir. Sorry, sir. Well, it's probably nothing, but we were trying to get the six o'clock news. On the radio."

"And?"

"And it isn't there."

The sergeant gawked. "Constable Meadows, have you come in here interrupting a peer of the realm to tell us that, in your professional opinion, someone has stolen the BBC's six o'clock news?"

Meadows gulped. "Well, not exactly, sir. I mean, the news isn't there, but something else is. All we can tune to, on any frequency, is some kid calling for a Scotland Yard inspector called Drake. He says he's trapped in the Crystal Palace with some other kids and soldiers." Meadows looked from his bemused sergeant to Charlie's grave expression, then to Art, who knew he was grinning despite the seriousness of the situation. "The kid's name," he added, "is Jonny Levin."

Sarah seemed amused at Arthur's surprise.

"I thought you'd worked it out," she said. "I thought, when I told you I had somewhere quiet I can escape to when I want to work, that you'd realize. Didn't you hear me call out to you the other day?"

"That was you?" Arthur tried to recall how the voice had sounded—how it had been echoed and distorted by the shape of the house, by his own fear and surprise.

Sarah went over to the table. Arthur tracked her with the flashlight as she sat down and looked at her books. "So how did you know about this place?" she asked. "I suppose you followed me after the fireworks?"

He nodded. "And I knew about it from the casebook," he admitted.

She was frowning. "What casebook?"

"The Invisible Detective's casebook."

This seemed to surprise her, and Arthur found he was amused and pleased at the reversal.

"I never heard of any casebook," she confessed. "But it might help."

"Help?"

"With the website, of course." Sarah stood up again. "Since I asked that idiot student teacher at Computer Club for advice on the scripting, he's been telling everyone about this wonderful site where you get your questions answered."

Arthur frowned. "I thought it was all automatic. It says about artificial intelligence and search engines and stuff."

"Yeah," Sarah said. "Right. Me and my online encyclopedia more like. Have you any idea how long it takes to find stuff out and paste it into an e-mail?"

"But you knew about the Shadow Beast," Arthur protested. "That's not in any encyclopedia." He wanted to tell her he had met the beast, that he and Grandad had come face-to-face with it. "Nor is the Invisible Detective."

"That's why I was surprised you knew about him. But your dad knew my dad before he went away, so I suppose . . ."

Suppose what? Arthur wanted to ask. But he didn't. Instead he stood absolutely still, straining to hear. There was a sound from downstairs, he was sure. Someone moving around perhaps.

Sarah was also listening, frowning. "Did you hear that?" she whispered.

"Downstairs," he hissed back.

She seemed to take this as a suggestion, pushing past Arthur and walking quietly along the landing. He followed her, and together they peered cautiously over the banisters and down into the hallway below.

Nothing.

The noise was louder now. It sounded like a struggle—a fight.

"It's coming from the cellar," Arthur said.

Sarah nodded. She bit at her lower lip as she seemed to consider. "Come on, then," she said. "Let's see who's down there."

CHAPTER 12

Art could see the Crystal Palace, one end of it illuminated from within by a dull red glow. It had not been difficult to slip through the police cordon and into the park. He ran, breathless, to the main entrance. The doors seemed to have gone and there was broken glass everywhere. The whole place was eerily silent.

He was standing in the entranceway, wondering where to go, what to do, when a sudden sound made him turn—footsteps crunching on broken glass.

It was Charlie.

"I'm going in there. I'm going to find them," Art said defiantly.

Charlie nodded. "I know. They're in the south tower, according to Jonny." He led the way into the huge building.

"They contacted your father," Charlie said as they hurried along the main concourse. "He's liaising with the War Office and bringing in reinforcements. Then they'll close in."

"That will be too late."

Charlie nodded. "Yes, I'm afraid it may." There was a deep sadness in his eyes as he paused and turned to Art. "Tell me what happened to Algie," he said.

It had gone quiet outside. The only sound was Jonny's repeated message into the microphone that he and Ted had connected to the damaged radio-telephone and various other bits of equipment they had salvaged.

"We are trapped in the south tower of the Crystal Palace and need help urgently," Jonny said again. "I repeat, this is a message for the War Office or the police, or Captain Maltravers's army unit. . . ."

"Why's it so quiet outside?" Meg asked Sergeant Barker in a low voice. "What are they up to?"

Barker shrugged. "I don't know. But I think we should find out." He beckoned Flinch over. "I'm going to lift you as high as I can," he told her. "See if you can scramble up enough to get a quick look outside, OK?"

Flinch nodded.

"Good girl." Barker heaved her up onto his shoulders, his knees bending to take the weight. As he straightened, the girl climbed up so she was standing on his shoulders, then leaned forward against the wall over the door.

"It's too smooth. I can't get a grip." She stared down at them, disappointed. Then Flinch's face cleared. "Have you got a knife?"

"Jimmy?" Barker called to the soldier. "Knife."

Jimmy had a bayonet in his belt and passed it up to Flinch. Barker almost lost his balance as she reached down for it. Then she straightened up again and stabbed the blade hard into the wall as high up as she could reach.

It sliced easily into the partition wall and Flinch was able to lever herself up on the end of the bayonet that remained jutting out. She was falling already, toppling backward as she managed to crane her neck out and look quickly over the top of the wall.

Then she fell. Barker caught her and lowered her the final few feet to the floor.

Flinch was breathless. "They got grenades," she gasped. "Putting them up against the door."

"They're going to blow their way in."

"That man's out there with them. I think he's in charge. With the silver-topped cane."

"Lawson," Meg said.

"Never mind about him." Barker pulled Jonny away from the microphone. "And never mind about that. People have either heard or they haven't. Under cover, quick."

With Jimmy and Ted's help, Barker tipped over the workbench, sending equipment, glass and components flying. Then he shoved Flinch, Meg and Jonny behind the makeshift barricade.

"As soon as the door blows," he said, "we have to get out of here—surprise them with our speed. Can you do that?"

Jonny was grinning. "I can," he said.

A second later, the door exploded inward with a blast of sound. Glass was rattling in sympathy outside, and the workbench shifted a foot across the floor under the impact. Smoke poured over the top, stinging Meg's eyes and catching in her throat.

"Right," Barker shouted. "Go!"

Jonny was already on his feet, dragging Flinch with him as he dashed for the smoke-filled doorway. There were shadowy shapes on the other side, but Meg ignored them, tried not to think what they might be as she put her head down and charged through. Her shoulder caught something on the way and she heard a rasping grunt of surprise. Another dark shape loomed in front of her.

Behind her Barker was shouting and Jimmy's rifle cracked out a shot. The shape fell away. Meg was out of the smoke now, could see Jonny and Flinch running ahead of her—back toward the main concourse and out of the tower.

She risked a glance behind. Barker was close on her heels, but behind him she could see the dark shape of one of the ghost soldiers as it aimed its rifle. She froze in horror, unable even to call out a warning.

Then suddenly the creature was sprawling headlong as Jimmy shouldered it aside, kicking the rifle away from its clutching fingers. He grabbed Meg by the arm as he raced past her, dragging her after him.

The corridor forked. Jonny was already pulling Flinch one way.

"We'll try to draw them off," Barker shouted from behind Meg. "Jimmy, stay with the kids, look after them. Ted, you're with me."

Meg turned in time to see Sergeant Barker and Ted pause at the entrance to the other corridor, waiting to be sure the ghost soldiers saw—and followed—them.

They kept running. Meg could hear the ghost soldiers behind them in the smoke. She could hear Lawson shouting at them to follow and realized that they were not after all following Barker and Ted. They were heading for the main entrance—following Meg and the others, and ready to cut off any escape. Her face was wet, streaming with tears from the smoke, or perhaps from fear, or from the effort of running.

Meanwhile, Jonny and Flinch slowed to allow the others to catch up. Together, the four of them rounded the corner and emerged into the main concourse. At the front of the group, Jonny let out a cry of surprise and skidded to a halt. He almost knocked into a figure at the side of the corridor—but it was only the mannequin of the cricketer in full whites, padded up and holding a bat. The other side of the large doorway was the footballer. Waxworks. The room beyond was dark, but Meg thought she could make out vague shapes standing in the gloom.

In front of her, through the lingering wisps of smoke, lit by the dull moonlight that shone through the vaulted glass ceiling, Meg could see two figures in the main concourse.

"We can't go back," Jimmy said.

"We don't need to, Jimmy," Flinch gasped, breathless. "It's Art and Charlie."

But what she had not seen, but which Meg and the others had noticed, was a line of figures arriving behind their two friends. A line of four skull-faced soldiers that was marching inexorably toward them.

. . .

Art's relief at seeing Jonny, Flinch and Meg with the soldier Flinch had called Jimmy evaporated as he realized they were looking past him and Charlie. He turned slowly, aware that Charlie was mirroring the movement.

And behind him he saw the four ghost soldiers that were slowly approaching. Three of them held rifles, the fourth—slightly ahead of the others and in captain's uniform—a revolver. Even in the dim light, Art could make out that his face was less ratlike than that of the others. It still clung to its last vestiges of humanity.

"Algie?" Charlie breathed. "Oh, Algie—what have they done to you?"

Algie's expression did not change. He stopped in front of them, raising his revolver in one hand and bringing the other up to steady his aim. The soldier with Jonny, Meg and Flinch pointed his rifle at the creature Algie had become.

Jonny was turning to run, but Art could see that another half-dozen or so ghost soldiers were rapidly closing in on them. Lawson was running with them, looking smug and satisfied. They were trapped between the two groups. Resigned, Art put his hands up. If they could stall matters long enough for Dad to arrive with reinforcements, they might yet escape.

But Lawson had other ideas. "Excellent," he said as he stood before them, waving for the ghost soldiers to spread out. "Prepare to execute them."

In reply, Jimmy swung around, moving his rifle from Algie so that it pointed at Lawson.

"One shot, mate," he said, "and you get it first."

Lawson looked worried. Then he smiled again. "Not if we shoot you first," he said quietly. Even as he finished speaking, a shot cracked out and Jimmy dropped his rifle with a yelp of pain. Blood leaked from his wounded hand and Meg ran to bind it with a handkerchief.

Algie's revolver moved back to cover Charlie.

"How very appropriate," Lawson said. "Captain Maltravers, you and your men will form the firing squad."

Algie's voice, barely recognizable, was a low, guttural snarl: "Take aim."

The three ghost soldiers with him raised their rifles.

"Wait," Charlie pleaded. "Think about what you're doing, Algie. Think about who you are. Think about what they have done to you." But there was no indication that his nephew could hear him. "Think about what they have done to all of you. What they will keep on doing if we don't stop them. How many more people must suffer for this insane experiment?"

Algie blinked. It was not much, but perhaps it meant he could at least hear Charlie's words.

"We can stop them," Art said. "We can make sure no one else suffers like you. No one else dies."

Was it Art's imagination or did the revolver dip slightly? It was impossible to tell.

"You will obey your orders," Lawson shouted. He

raised his cane and brandished it like a flag, rallying his troops. "Execute them," he snarled. His face twisted into a grotesque smile as he looked directly at Meg and then Art. "Women and children first."

"You can't," Jimmy shouted back. He dived headlong, scrabbling for his fallen rifle.

The sudden movement seemed to prompt Algie into action. "Take aim," he grunted again, bringing up his revolver.

Jimmy had his rifle now, but his hand snagged in the strap as he tried to raise it.

"Algie!" Charlie shouted.

Flinch hid her face in her hands. Jonny looked white and drawn. Meg stood defiant, hands on her hips. Art swallowed, his mouth and throat dry.

Algie paused and looked at the three ghost soldiers beside him. They returned his gaze through red, sunken eyes, acknowledging their orders.

"Fire!"

The guns moved surprisingly quickly as they were trained on their selected targets. Algie moved first, the revolver coming around in an arc. Its shot preceded those of the rifles by a split second—a staccato whip-crack of sound. The ghost soldier standing beside Lawson dropped immediately.

A moment later, three other ghost soldiers behind Lawson crashed to the floor as the bullets reached their new targets.

Jimmy had his rifle aimed now and a fifth ghost soldier reeled backward, arms flailing as the bullet caught him.

But already the last two of Lawson's ghost soldiers were returning fire. Art dived for the floor, dragging Charlie with him. He rolled over to see that Jonny and Meg had followed. Flinch was sheltering behind the life-sized model of a cricketer set up beside a wide doorway.

Algie's revolver cracked again and another of Lawson's ghost soldiers fell. But two of Algie's were also dead. Another shot and only Algie was left. His revolver swung to point directly at Lawson. Art saw the man's eyes widen in horror and fright.

Click.

Lawson dropped to his knees and at first Art thought he had been shot despite the lack of noise. But Algie was out of ammunition and Lawson was pulling something from the pocket of one of the fallen creatures. He stood up again, holding whatever it was in both hands, pulling at it.

It was a grenade.

Algie was reloading. But his movements were measured, mechanical—too slow.

Lawson drew back his arm and threw.

Art was moving before he knew what he was doing, staggering toward Flinch, almost losing his balance and falling against the cricketer. His hands closed on the wooden handle as he grabbed it, turned, lashed out.

The grenade was heavy. The impact of it colliding with

the cricket bat sent shivers up Art's arm and jarred his elbow. But he had struck it in the center of the bat—the sweet spot. The grenade looped back the way it had come and Art dived for the floor again, hands over the back of his head.

The grenade exploded in midair, right above the incredulous Lawson. Out of the corner of his eye, Art saw the man's body hurled backward. The last of his ghost soldiers caught the edge of the blast and collapsed in a heap. Lawson crashed against a pair of dark velvet curtains that framed an alcove. One of the curtains broke free and fell, dragging over a tall display case that crashed and shattered to the ground, extending the sound of the explosion. One half of a silver-topped cane clattered down beside Lawson's lifeless body and spun to a halt among the shards of glittering glass.

The curtains had caught a spark from the explosion. One of them was immediately a pool of fire around Lawson's body. Flames seemed to run up the other curtain toward the high glass roof. As they reached the top, they leaped and spat across to other flammable material.

More curtains, parts of displays, even the ceiling itself seemed to be on fire. The footballer across the wide doorway was burning, like a candle. The football escaped from under his boot and rolled, burning, into the exhibition hall. As it went, it left a fiery trail and, one after another, the waxwork figures started to glisten, melt and burn. . . .

There was a dull cracking sound and a single pane of glass dropped from the ceiling and exploded on the floor close to where Art was staggering to his feet.

"Let's get out of here," Jimmy shouted.

"The whole place will go up once those waxworks catch light," Charlie said. "Quick—while we can still see."

Thick, oily black smoke was billowing out of the hall and through the concourse. Art was already choking and coughing. He pulled Flinch to her feet, checked that Jonny and Meg were with them, and hurried back toward the main entrance.

The fire was hot on his back as Art ran. He was astonished it was spreading so quickly. He paused only to check that he knew where everyone was, that nobody was getting left behind. Jonny was out in front, of course. Before long they were splashing through the circular pond inside the main doors, not bothering to try to run around it.

Then, outside.

"We need to get well away," Art gasped as he caught his breath. Again he looked around, mentally counting. He could see Jimmy slapping another soldier on the back, while a burly sergeant watched and laughed and choked on the acrid smoke.

"Where's Algie?" Charlie asked.

But Art hardly heard him. Where was Flinch? He could see from Meg's expression that she too had realized the girl was no longer with them.

Without a word, they both turned and plunged back

into the Crystal Palace. The smoke was so thick now, they could see almost nothing.

"Flinch!" Art shouted. "Where are you, Flinch?"

Meg was calling too. And after what seemed like forever, Art heard the answering call. "I'm here. Nearly finished."

"Finished?" Meg muttered. "What's she doing?"

Art grabbed Meg's arm, holding on so as not to lose her as they made their way through the thick darkness toward Flinch's voice.

"Are you lost? We're over here," he shouted.

"Do you need help, Flinch?" Meg called.

"No, I managed." Flinch's voice was quiet, and Art realized she was right beside him in the smoke. She was holding something, but he could not see what.

"Where were you?" he demanded.

She sounded indignant as they emerged once again into the fresh night air. In the distance a clock was chiming eight o'clock. "I had to get a bucket," Flinch explained.

Jonny had joined them. He looked relieved, but pale beneath a grimy covering of soot. Art expected he looked much the same. "A bucket?" Jonny said with a nervous laugh. "You won't put this fire out with a bucket."

"Not for the fire," Flinch told him. "This was all I could find." She held up a soldier's helmet for them to see. It had water in it, Art could see in the red glow from the flames. Something else too—something moving, something alive.

"For the goldfish. I couldn't leave them, could I?"

Their nervous laughter was joined by the distant bells of the first fire engines.

They watched the fire from Anerley Hill. The flames were enormous. Art reckoned they might be five hundred feet high, and he later heard that the fire could be seen from planes over the English Channel. At one point a flock of birds flew out of the main entrance of the Crystal Palace—moments before it collapsed. From the aviary, Charlie told them.

Ironically, the south tower was saved. But it was midnight before the hundreds of firemen even began to look as if they were in control. And by then most of the Crystal Palace was gone. From where Art and the others sat at the front of a gathering crowd of onlookers, the heat was almost unbearable.

Close to midnight, Flinch and Meg left for a few minutes to seek out a policeman they could charge with finding a new home for the goldfish. Jonny had convinced the girls it was not a good idea just to release them in the river.

The four of them were still there the next morning as the ruins smoldered on. Charlie had left during the night, to sort out some "official business," but he returned as dawn was breaking—with Art's dad.

"Enjoying the fireworks?" Dad asked. But his face was grim. "A tragic loss," he said with a sigh. "Lord Fothering-ton has been at pains to assure me that all this has nothing to do with you lot," he added in a quiet voice, so that only the Cannoniers could hear him. "Somehow that does little to reassure me." Then he smiled thinly. "Be that as it may, come with me and I'll show you what's left of the place."

They spent a while walking around the blackened, skeletal remains of the ironwork structure with Art's dad and Charlie.

"Eighty-eight fire engines," Dad told them, "from four brigades. Over four hundred firemen."

"A lot of police too," Meg said.

"They are here for other reasons as well," Charlie pointed out. "And I don't just mean crowd control." He nodded meaningfully.

"Yes, 750 police officers," Art's dad said. He was looking across the park, away from the burned-out remains of the palace. "And one of them," he said, "is a photographer. How about a picture of the Cannoniers on this historic morning?"

Art wasn't sure he felt like being photographed, not after the events of the previous night. But he smiled thinly and said nothing.

"Will you be in it?" Flinch asked Charlie, as Art's dad went to organize the photograph.

"I have rather a lot to do," Charlie told her gently. "And you don't want an old codger like me in your photograph, now do you?"

"Of course we do," Meg assured him.

"Nevertheless . . ." Charlie held his hands up to forestall further argument. "I shall see you all soon, I'm sure."

"You're going to look for Algie, aren't you?" Art said quietly.

Charlie nodded. "The house and the underground base are deserted, I'm told. Miss Gibson is gone, which is a worry. I doubt if we shall ever know what happened to Algie, but I owe it to him to try to find out."

He turned, and together they looked back at the remains of the Crystal Palace. Then Charlie tipped his hat and walked stiffly away.

The sounds were indeed coming from the cellar. Arthur could tell as soon as he opened the door and shone his flashlight down the steep stone steps. Sarah had a flashlight as well, and together they made their way carefully down the stairs.

It was empty. They both flashed their flashlights around the whitewashed walls—nothing.

And yet they could still hear the sounds. They were muffled but audible. It was the sound of a fight. If Arthur strained, he thought he could hear two voices shouting at each other. One was a woman's, he was sure. The other was more of a low grunt, noises rather than words.

"There's nobody here," Sarah said incredulously.

"Perhaps they're in the secret base."

"That's sealed up. My dad told me," Sarah said. Her face

was pale against her dark hair as Arthur's flashlight swept over it. "But the government still owns the house, he said. That's how I knew it would stay empty. Official secrets or something."

"If they're not in the base . . ." Arthur looked around again, struggling to understand what he was hearing. As he turned, he was aware of the weight in his coat and instinctively he put his hand inside his pocket. He could feel the clock. The raised edge of the winding key grazed his fingers and he grasped it—pulled at it, as he thought.

It was like focusing an image projected on the wall. One moment there was just the sounds, the next shadows. Then slowly, as the sounds became more distinct, the shadows seemed to coalesce into figures—two figures, facing each other on the other side of the cellar.

Sarah gasped with astonishment. "Ghosts."

"It's all right, they can't see us," Arthur said. But then he remembered how Charlie had spoken to him. "At least, I hope not."

But they seemed too intent on each other to notice they were being watched from another time. One was a woman— her hair cropped short and her nose a vicious beak overhanging a thin, cruel mouth. But the other figure, while male, was barely a man. He was in uniform, but his face was drawn, the eyes sunken, his breathing a heavy rasp.

"The redoubtable Captain Maltravers," the woman said, her voice as thin as her mouth. "How goes the battle?"

The soldier's voice was a guttural slur of words that

seemed an effort to him. "You have lost. Lawson is dead. It's over."

The woman laughed. "Over? I haven't begun yet. Perhaps a change of sponsor, but the experiments will continue." She thrust her face close to Algie's. "I'm told Berlin is very pleasant this time of year." She pushed him away and he staggered, almost falling.

"Never," he gasped back.

"And who is going to stop me? You can hardly stand up. Hydraulics need tuning, I expect." She laughed again and took a step forward.

But the soldier was in front of her. She tried to push him away again, but this time he kept his balance.

"What's happening?" Sarah hissed.

"It's Algie," Arthur realized. "And Miss Gibson."

Sarah stared at him blankly, confused, but suddenly Arthur knew what was about to happen, how this would end.

She tried to push Algie aside once more. But this time he grabbed her wrists and started to drag her with him toward the stairs. "Taking you to Uncle Charlie," he gasped through his jutting jaw. His long teeth caught the flashlight's beam, even though he could not see it.

Miss Gibson tried to pull away, got one hand free, then stamped at Algie's feet. She managed to drag him back toward an alcove, and Arthur could see that Algie's strength was weakening. He lost his grip on her other hand and, with a cry of triumph, Miss Gibson locked both her hands around his throat. Algie pulled and tore at them, but she was not going to let him go now.

"Finished, am I?" she snarled, her face contorted with the effort.

Algie's eyes were wide as he fought for breath. He was against the wall now, slipping down as he lost consciousness. With one weak hand, he reached out toward her face, trying to push her away. With the other . . .

Arthur watched Algie's pawlike hand close on the iron ring in the wall. Saw it pull and the ring move. Watched as the wall swung open behind him and he fell backward, pulling Miss Gibson after him. The two of them crashed into the wooden shelves in the concealed cupboard, sending several of them crashing to the floor as they fought.

Algie was forced down to his knees, but already the door was swinging shut again on its hinge. Miss Gibson seemed not to have noticed, but Algie had. He was pulling her right into the cupboard, so that the door could latch shut behind her.

Another shelf collapsed, tipping its contents off as it angled, then fell. Algie was scrabbling, grabbing, grasping at whatever he could find on the floor as he was forced down, searching for something to use as a weapon. Then Arthur's vision seemed to shimmer and distort, and the door closed with a dull click.

"Come on," Sarah said quietly. "It's time we were going."

He had no chance to talk to Sarah for the next few days at school. Once the ghosts had gone, once Algie and Miss Gibson were dead, Sarah and Arthur had left the house with barely a word to each other.

Arthur had waited while Sarah gathered her books and schoolwork. Then they had let themselves out of the house into the deserted street. They caught a bus from the next road, sitting in silence for most of the way home.

"Does your casebook say what happened?" Sarah asked eventually.

Arthur shook his head. "They didn't know. Not what we saw. But everything else is in it."

"Can I . . ." She hesitated as the bus slowed for a bend. "Can I see it sometime?"

Arthur was not sure about this. It was his book. His and Art's—Grandad's. He didn't know if anyone else should see it, if anyone else was meant to.

"This is my stop," he said.

CHAPTER 13

There was an air of hushed expectancy in the darkened room. Everyone—including Meg, Jonny and Flinch—was waiting for the Invisible Detective to speak.

"Last Monday," he said at last, "was a historic day."

The silence seemed to get even deeper. It seemed as if all the people in the room were holding their breath. Behind the curtain, Jonny put his hand on Meg's shoulder without even realizing. Without even realizing, she did not push it away as she in turn put her arm around Flinch and they all listened.

"It was the first time that I have been unable to attend one of these consulting sessions. And I apologize to all of you who came along expecting to find me here. Unfortunately, I was otherwise detained." The detective seemed to make a point of clearing his throat. "I cannot tell you the details of where I was or what I was doing, as that is a matter of national security."

The silence was broken by gasps of astonishment and awe.

"But," the detective continued, "suffice to say that you will all know of another historic event last Monday night in London."

There were mutterings at this. Everyone knew about the fire that had destroyed the Crystal Palace. Several people had seen the flames.

"You can rest assured that it will take an event of that magnitude to interrupt our future meetings," the detective went on. "And I can say no more than that I was indeed involved in certain 'events' last Monday night and witnessed them at rather closer quarters than was comfortable. Now, let us move on. . . ."

As the buzz of whispered speculation gathered volume, Meg shrugged Jonny's hand from her shoulder. Flinch shuffled her feet, already getting bored. Jonny grinned in the near darkness at Meg's stern expression. And the Invisible Detective, his reputation even more enhanced, prepared once more to astonish and amaze his audience.

Grandad had a yellowed copy of the *Daily Mirror* open on his knee. The front-page headline was "Fire Wrecks Crystal Palace: Royal Duke Watches." There was a black-and-white photo—the remains of the dark skeleton of the palace silhouetted against the fire.

"That wasn't Charlie," Grandad said, tapping the headline with a gnarled finger. "The Duke of Kent. I think Charlie knew him." He looked up at Art. "Some people saw us coming out, you know. Dad put it about we were members of the orchestra." He gave a short laugh. "It says in here that the goldfish died." His eyes were shining with amusement. "Don't believe everything you read in the papers."

"I don't." Arthur sighed. "It's a pity we can't go back and tell them what happened to Algie. Now we know. I mean, go back and tell you, back then."

Grandad frowned. "But you can," he said quietly. He looked puzzled at Arthur's startled expression. "We spoke often, you and I. Don't you remember?"

Arthur shook his head. "No," he said in bewilderment. "No, I don't."

"Perhaps we haven't done it yet," Grandad murmured. "I get so confused about time. But surely you must remember? That's why you have the clock."